D

Bones

Deadly Bones

Matthew Smith-Wise

Deadly Bones
DCI Kate Melrose: Book 1

For KW, with love –
thank you for all your support

1

'I've always been obsessed with the dead. I was only eight when I dug up my first skeleton. I was in the garden of our family home, having just excitedly unwrapped a set of bright red digging tools for my birthday. I donned my fedora, the influence of a certain fictional archaeologist, I marked out my dig site with some wooden ice lolly sticks and string, then I commenced the excavation of our much-lamented dog, Rupert. From that day I knew that I wanted to dig up fossils for a living. I've been fortunate that my job has taken me to so many amazing countries and I've been privileged to play a part in some of the biggest archaeological discoveries of my generation.'

As Professor Malcolm Hail paused to take a sip of water from the tumbler glass resting on the podium in front of him, there was a scattering of polite applause from the audience. He looked out at the sea of faces before him; a mixture of colleagues or patrons from the museum and members of the public who had entered a ballot to be among the first to be at the opening of this new exhibition.

In a neat row along the back, the PR team had arranged a handful of journalists and photographers; most were representatives of the two biggest local newspapers, but they had also managed to attract one national. The sound of intermittent clicks from the shutters of the cameras echoed throughout the vast entrance hall of the Museum of Natural History, all capturing the professor in front of the imposing figure of a triceratops. The full-size replica stood proudly in the middle of the room, its head gazing upon the upper-level balcony, horns thrust proudly towards the skylight.

Professor Hail was always present at the opening of a new exhibition – he had spent the past three years as Head of Palaeontology at the museum and his name was still a draw in the world of natural history. He had always firmly believed that any publicity or attention that he could help bring to the museum was worthwhile. Malcolm placed the glass back down on the podium before turning over to the next page of his speech.

'Today I'm pleased and proud to have been asked to unveil the latest exhibition here at our wonderful Museum of Natural History in Spiral Bay. This exhibition is the collaborative work of a number of people, not only here but also at museums throughout the country, and indeed the world.'

Professor Hail was interrupted by the sound of the main door to the museum swinging open and quickly slamming shut. A loud clunk echoed throughout the hall as the wooden panel connected with the frame. Professor Hail looked up from his notes and impatiently tapped the podium as he watched a bearded man with glasses scurry forward to a seat on the back row.

A few members of the audience shuffled in their seats, tutting in disgust, whilst others turned to catch a glance of the inconsiderate latecomer. Professor Hail gathered the pages of his speech in his hands and shuffled them together. He meticulously aligned each sheet into a tidy stack, before placing them down and continuing from where he had been rudely interrupted.

'This fantastic new collection brings together the greatest discoveries of all time and after a six week stay with us, everything will be safely packed away and sent on a one-year tour around the UK, before embarking upon its much-anticipated international journey, involving eight countries. Not only does this exhibition provide an important educational and interactive resource, it's also a lot of fun for all ages, with plenty of opportunities for a 'hands on' experience. When I had a peek earlier at all the items and activities that they've got in store for you, suddenly beneath my tweed jacket and elbow pads, I was that kid again with the red spade.'

The audience gently laughed as Professor Hail stepped down from the podium and walked over to a closed door at the side of the hall. Next to the stone archway stood a woman holding a large pair of scissors.

'Thank you, Edith; our wonderful Museum Director, ladies and gentlemen.'

The professor clapped softly as he spoke these words, before taking the scissors and lifting them up towards a ribbon that stretched across the width of the doorway.

'Without any further delay, I give you: "Finding Fossils".'

The scissor blades sliced through the red material as flashes from the cameras began to fill the room like an explosive firework display. The audience rose to their feet, applauding and cheering. The late guest remained seated, his arms tightly folded, his eyes sternly peering through the gaps in the crowd in the direction of the Head of Palaeontology.

Professor Hail placed the scissors down on a small table and shook hands with Edith as they smiled in the direction of the photographers, before pushing open the door to the exhibition and stepping inside. The eager group of onlookers were quick to follow, moving as one towards the entrance and beginning to funnel themselves through the doorway, leaving only the disgruntled man behind, alone.

During the next few hours, the exhibition room was buzzing with the sounds of excited chatter. Some of the visitors decided to take a more structured approach, methodically working their way through from start to finish, digesting each and every word on the display boards; others skim read the information as they rushed along, eagerly seeking out the various hands-on activities available.

Professor Hail slowly navigated his way around the many sections, making sure he stopped to talk with everyone he passed. He knew the importance of PR, particularly for a museum with no government funding. This was a place that relied heavily on sponsorship and the footfall through the doors each day.

'Miss Da Silva,' called Professor Hail, walking over to a tall lady who was stood by one of the displays near the entrance. As she turned and smiled, a redness spread in her cheeks that matched the colour of her shoulder length hair and betrayed a shyness she had always tried to keep a secret. She held out her slender arm, offering him her hand.

'How many times must I tell you to call me Laura?'

Professor Hail took her hand in his and smiled. 'Thank you for coming along today, Laura, particularly on a Saturday. Are you planning to bring your class here at some point?'

'Yes, I'm just finalising the details for a trip at the moment. To get final sign off from the school I needed to come along and check out the exhibition myself. It's really great, I think they're going to love it.'

'I'm glad you approve,' Professor Hail smiled. 'Let me know when you're planning on bringing them here and I'll clear my diary and give you a personal tour, if you'd like.'

'That would be wonderful, thank you. How about I send you an email once I get the green light?'

'Perfect. If you'll excuse me, there's a few more people I need to talk to.'

Professor Hail smiled and nodded, before turning away and heading across to Edith, who was reading a display board. In the middle of the room, he passed a museum assistant handing out flutes of champagne from a silver tray. As he walked by, he picked up two of the glasses and moved over to where the museum director was stood. Throughout the professor's short journey, Laura had remained in the same place like a statue, eagerly watching his every move.

'Here you go, Edith, drink this.'

'Thank you, Malcolm.'

She took a few sips out of politeness, before holding the glass in her hand, tapping the base nervously with her fingernails as she looked around the room.

'It's been a success, Director, don't look so worried.' The professor put his hand on her shoulder as he spoke.

'Yes, it has, the turnout has been fantastic. With so much bad publicity following all these break-ins, we just really need some good news.'

'I know,' Professor Hail nodded understandingly. 'Actually, as we're on the subject of bad publicity, I think I may have uncovered something. I just need to…'

The professor was interrupted midway through his sentence by the arrival of Georgie Westbrook, the collections co-ordinator for the museum.

'This is a resounding triumph,' she beamed, stopping between Edith and Malcolm and glancing over her right shoulder to soak in some more of the atmosphere.

'Well done, Georgie, you've put a lot of hours into this.'

'We all have, Director, it's been a true team effort. On top of all this, Malcolm here still found the time to write a book as well!'

Edith turned to the professor. 'Congratulations, Malcolm, I didn't realise you had finished, that's some accomplishment. You must hardly sleep to be able to get so much done.'

'I'll have plenty of time for sleep when I'm dead,' joked the professor.

'When will it hit the shelves?' said Edith.

'I've got a proof copy on my desk as we speak. I just need to sign off on it and then it'll be out in print pretty soon.'

'And, it's managed to upset Professor Stone, so it's a double win,' laughed Georgie, before drinking her remaining champagne and shaking the glass gently to highlight its emptiness. 'Well, I'd better get a refill. I'll catch up with you both later.'

Professor Hail and Edith both watched as Georgie walked away. She had worn a tight black dress that sat just above her knees and showcased her toned body and long legs. Being one of the younger members of staff, she was a bit less conservative about her work attire, but everyone knew not to let her playful side fool them. Georgie had a brilliant mind and had risen through the ranks quickly at several other museums, prior to joining them here.

'I thought I saw Professor Stone earlier,' said Edith, turning back to Professor Hail.

'Yes, he walked in late, surprise, surprise! I thought he was going to make a nuisance of himself, but thankfully he just sat at the back glaring at me. I've been waiting for the inevitable confrontation since, but he seems to have disappeared.' The professor paused to look around the room for a few moments, before turning back to Edith. 'Anyway, I'm going to carry on mingling a bit more. I'm not letting that old fool ruin our day.'

He clinked his glass with the director's and nodded before continuing on his journey through the exhibition, leaving Edith behind, still nervously tapping her glass.

By the time the evening was winding to a close, Professor Hail had relocated to the main door of the museum. He had taken it upon himself to fulfil the role of cloakroom assistant and was fetching the coats and hats of the visitors before bidding each of them a safe journey home.

When the last of the guests had gone, the professor stepped back inside the entrance to Finding Fossils and sat down on a bench looking out among the many artefacts, displays and fossils housed within the collection. For the next hour or so, he was transported back to his childhood. He could feel the wooden handle of the red spade in his hand, the curved steel head glistening in the sunlight as he walked down the family garden to his chosen digging site.

He remembered how the grass and soil felt as he sifted it through his hands for the first time and the emotions that ran through him when he made his discovery. Ever since that day his hobby, his job, reminded him of his own mortality – that there had been life before and it would continue long after his own body had been claimed by the land.

Professor Hail was brought back to reality by two beeps of his watch. He glanced down at the dials and saw it was now ten o'clock. As he passed through the Great Hall, the professor paused to look at the intimidating figure of the triceratops. Despite the dim light, the skeleton cast a sinister shadow across him.

He was about to continue his journey towards the staircase that led to his office, when the sound of footsteps caught his attention, causing him to look back towards the main entrance of the museum.

'Goodnight, Edith, and well done today. This exhibition is a demonstration of what can be achieved when museums collaborate. The fact that the tour begins here is a testament to you and your hard work to continually put us on the map.'

'Thank you, Malcolm. I'm grateful for all your support today. You said something earlier about some news you wanted to share, but you didn't get to finish.'

'Ah, that. It's probably best I don't say anything more at this moment in time. I don't want to give any misinformation, but I'm following up on a hunch and if I'm correct, I'll tell you everything in a few days.'

'Please be careful. Max is the night guard on duty, so call him if you need anything.'

'That's reassuring,' laughed Professor Hail. 'I'm being protected by the one person who was actually alive during the reign of the dinosaurs.'

'He is not that old,' scoffed Edith. 'Goodnight and don't work too late now, will you?'

The professor smiled and saluted before continuing up the stairs and along the upper balcony towards his office. Edith chuckled to herself as she buttoned up her jacket and stepped out into the cold night air, the heavy door slamming behind her.

Once inside his office, the professor walked behind a large oak desk and turned on a green lamp to his left, before sitting down. He swivelled in his chair to face a cabinet behind him and opened the top compartment. He pulled out a small glass and a bottle of rum, holding one in each hand as he spun back to face the desk.

As the professor placed the two items down onto the wooden surface, a feeling of panic and horror overcame him. For a moment, he did not move. Instead, he remained seated, staring without a single blink at the vacant space on his desk that had previously been occupied by the proof copy of his book.

Like a whirlwind, he began furiously scattering papers across the floor, sweeping his arms from left to right as he stood up from the chair. Each drawer was pulled mercilessly out along its runners and then dropped unsupported to the ground, landing with a series of thuds. He was so invested in the frantic search that he had not noticed the arrival of Max in the doorway.

'Professor! Is everything alright? I was just patrolling one of the upper galleries and heard noises coming from here. What's going on?'

'Max – do you know if anyone came into my office during the exhibition opening earlier?' As he spoke these words, the professor rushed over to where the guard stood in the doorway.

'I couldn't really say, sir, I only started my shift at 7 p.m. But no one has been up or down those stairs during that time. The first person was yourself as you were saying goodbye to the director a short while ago. What's going on, has there been another theft?'

'Yes, there most certainly has. And I think I know exactly who the culprit is.'

'Do you want me to call the police?'

'No, no, thank you, Max. I think I can deal with this one myself. Sorry for causing a disturbance. Please, carry on with your patrol.'

Max nodded his head and moved away from the dim light of the office and back into the darkened corridor. He took a torch from his utility belt and shone the beam out in front as he began walking back towards the staircase.

For a few moments, Professor Hail stood and watched as the light began to fade, until he could see no further than the length of his shadow, cast on the floor in front of him by the desk lamp. He slammed the door shut and marched over to the phone on his desk, lifting the receiver and punching in a set of numbers. The phone rang a few times before a connection was eventually made.

'Hello?'

The person on the other end was weary, their voice strained as if they had been awoken from a deep sleep.

'Did you really think you would get away with this?' Malcolm screamed down the phone, barely taking time for a breath. 'You really think because you've stolen it, that it'll stop me from going ahead and publishing it?'

'What the hell are you talking about?'

'I think you fucking well know what I'm talking about, so spare me your stupid act. This isn't over and this isn't going away. Deal with it!'

As the phone came crashing down, the plastic casing split into two pieces in the professor's hand. He looked down at them and as the rage within him took over, he turned and hurled them across the room, shattering the glass paned windows of the bookcase opposite.

Professor Hail moved back to the other side of the desk and poured himself a shot of rum, quickly grabbing the glass and tipping the entire contents down his throat in one gulp. He slammed the tumbler back onto the table and poured another shot, repeating the same process again. And again. And again.

Eventually, he sat down in his chair. The alcohol had tamed his fury. For a few moments he stared at the books through the shattered fragments of glass on the case opposite, then he crossed his arms on the desk to cushion his head and fell asleep.

***

Malcolm slowly opened his eyes, momentarily viewing his office at a blurry sideways glance before he gingerly lifted his head up and rubbed his face. Peering down at his watch he saw the time was now 2 a.m. There was a light pounding in his head, no doubt from the quick succession of rum shots.

As he stood up from his chair, his legs gave way slightly and he tumbled backwards, leaning onto the cabinet behind him to steady himself. The room began to spin around him and for a while he stood there, disorientated. After blinking a few times and running his hands across his forehead, he was able to focus his sight.

That's when he noticed the door to his office was wide open. Perhaps Max had been to check on him, spotted the open bottle of rum, seen him sleeping in an alcohol fuelled stupor and left him alone. Or perhaps there was someone else.

Malcolm was contemplating this disturbing thought when he heard the creak of a floorboard from the corridor outside. His entire body tensed. The hairs on his arms stood on end. He could feel the thumping of his heart, as if it were a creature trapped in a cage, trying to break free. He had to summon every ounce of courage to part his lips and utter a single word.

'Hello?'

He called timidly into the darkness, remaining where he stood. He didn't dare to move.

'Max? Is that you?'

No response. Just the overpowering dominance of silence. Perhaps the noise had been in his head; merely an after effect of the alcohol.

Like a new born child, the professor stepped out from behind the desk and began to reluctantly drag his feet towards the gaping hole of the doorway. He stopped just inside and cautiously leaned his head through. Nothing. Just the darkness.

'Max?'

Malcolm eventually gathered enough strength and crept forward through the doorway and turned left, walking out onto the balcony overlooking the Great Hall. Carefully, he peered over the edge, sliding the top half of his body across the wooden barrier until he was balancing on tiptoes, surveying the dark pit below.

The professor could just make out the tips of the

triceratops' horns, catching the moonlight. For a few moments he remained there, waiting for his eyes to adjust to the dark, unaware of the shadowy figure now stood behind him.

2

Paddington Station was almost deserted as I boarded the train at 04:50 this morning. I'm pretty sure there were more pigeons than passengers. Granted, it was early on a Sunday morning, but this is the city that never sleeps, supposedly. Nevertheless, walking through the empty carriages until I reached my reserved seat, I realised that I might be making the journey unaccompanied – to begin with anyway.

Despite being a semi-fast service, there were at least 10 stops in major towns and cities before I would arrive at my coastal destination. Plenty of time to gather my thoughts as I sped towards a new chapter in my life.

'Welcome aboard this 04:59 service to Spiral Bay, calling at...'

As the train guard listed the stations, I pushed my backpack onto the overhead shelf, then pulled my hair into a rough pony tail before I sat down and looked out onto the platform. Several more people had now arrived and were walking along the side of the train, glancing in every other window, searching for the perfect spot. A few of them were pulling small cases on wheels; others looked as though they were wearing the same clothes from the night before, no doubt on their way back from long hours of partying in the capital.

Over the far side of the station, one of the coffee wagons was opening up, which made me realise that I wasn't yet holding a cardboard cup full to the brim of caffeine for the journey ahead. That absence would need to be remedied when the onboard trolley came through. I'm used to working shifts, so the early start isn't much of an issue for me, but I definitely function better after a coffee. Perhaps accompanied by a warm croissant. And jam. A nice dollop of strawberry jam.

Four or five railway tracks across, a train had just pulled to a stop and a few passengers stepped out and hurried along to the barriers. London was slowly beginning to open its eyes after all. I wondered what the day would have in store for this vibrant collection of communities. I had worked and lived here for nearly 10 years now, but it was time for a change, a new direction, my own team.

I shifted around until I had settled on a comfier position in my seat and brought my attention back into the carriage. The interior looked fresh, as if this was a train on its maiden journey. Perhaps I wasn't the only one with new beginnings today. Trains have always been my favourite form of transport. Not only do they serve the practical purpose of taking a person from one place to another, without the need to sit in queues of polluted traffic or having to maintain the focus required to drive yourself. But, more importantly, they are gateways – to holidays, adventures, opportunities and so much more.

When I was a lot younger, our family holidays all began on a train. The journey became part of the holiday itself. My parents would book four seats with a table, so my sister and I could sit opposite one another and keep ourselves entertained by playing games. This would mostly involve cards, but occasionally we would have the treat of an actual board game. The most popular choice was something strategic, like chess. I've always enjoyed the challenge of thinking ahead and predicting your opponent's next move (a tactic that has proved useful in my line of work).

My Mum would usually sit quietly and read one of the many, many books she had brought along, back before they became available electronically. Although even now, when her and Dad go away, she still insists on taking a few real books with her. "There's something about the smell and feel of a book," she's always told me. We would only go away for a week but my Mum would have an entire bag dedicated to books. None of us ever believed she would get through them, but every year without fail, as the train would be pulling back into our home town, Mum would just be finishing the final page of the last book on her list.

Dad was content with sitting and watching the countryside racing past. Sometimes he would bring one of his train enthusiast magazines with him, but for most of the journey it would remain shut, playing a decorative role in our table's collage.

Every now and then he would sit forward suddenly, excitedly pointing out of the window, and start telling us some facts about the building, town or city we had just left behind. Despite my best intentions, it turns out that I had absorbed a lot of the information he was always throwing my way. And that wasn't limited to train journeys, oh no. I could be walking around the house and out of nowhere, Dad would appear and start spouting another piece of trivia. Not that I'm entirely ungrateful. Some of it has actually come in handy at work; other bits I've saved in what I call my 'scrapyard', for things such as pub quizzes, or the fiercely contested round of family games on Christmas Day.

To me, it still felt strange, even years later, being on a train without the other three sat with me. As we've grown older, priorities have shifted and as other aspects of life have taken over, we've shared those train journeys less, or with other people. Or, in my case, alone.

Moving on! Today isn't about dwelling on the past, no. Today is about looking towards a new future. Obviously, I'm nervous as hell, who wouldn't be on their first day? Every now and then the usual doubts set in – what if they don't like me? What if I don't like them? And worst of all – what if this is a huge mistake? These are all the types of thoughts that race through my mind. The ones I rarely tend to share out loud. I have spent years building up a reputation based on my strength and determination. I don't see the doubts as weaknesses, quite the opposite. But they are the more personal parts of me. Only I get to decide who sees the vulnerabilities and when. I hold the key to that door.

When I was offered the job at the end of my final interview, I was able to meet most of the team, so I will at least know some of their names. I've also had time to arrange a rented house a short drive from work and they've provided me with a car, which should be sat on the driveway waiting for me.

Living in London, I've not felt the desperate urge to own a vehicle, preferring to use the bus and tube. Or, if I was feeling energetic, I would sometimes run to work, taking a fairly scenic route through Hyde Park. Those days were few and far between, though, particularly during a pattern of unsocial shifts. I would find it easier to hit the gym before or after work, or on my days off, to keep up with my fitness. I'm not obsessed with body image, but it's important to me that I can run up a few flights of stairs and not be breathless at the top.

Having my accommodation sorted also means I've been able to ship most of my stuff ahead, which has also allowed me to indulge a little and take this nostalgic train journey rather than heading down in a van overcrowded with boxes. Although, it does mean that on arrival I have the rest of the day to tackle the unenviable task of unpacking the essential items that I'll need over the next week or so and getting things into some form of order before I start my first day tomorrow. I decided to leave it as late as possible before travelling down, to avoid sitting in a near empty house, in a town I'm unfamiliar with, talking myself out of a good career move.

During my second to last visit, I also discovered that one of my new neighbours, Rachel, is a close friend of someone from work, so I've given her a key to let the couriers in and check for any mail. This also meant that on my final 'pre-moving' trip there a week ago, I was able to entrust her with my cat, Chester. It might sound cruel, handing him over to someone he's never met before, but it would be no different to putting him in a cattery. I have pretty good instincts as well and, having met Rachel a couple of times now, she seems like someone I could get along with. Chester is also very laid back and he'll make friends with anyone that's shaking a packet of food at him. He has a gorgeous, fluffy, snow coloured coat, with a few hints of ginger scattered around. When his hair is all puffed up, he looks like a cloud walking along, or a pillow. I couldn't imagine making this move without him, so hopefully he'll like his new home. And hopefully I will too.

As the train began to move away, I craned my neck as much as possible to capture one last look at the concourse. I had built a lot of memories here and I had a feeling I would be back again to write another life chapter at some point. It didn't take us long to reach our top speed and within five minutes, London was a distant blob on the train app I was using to track my journey.

'Good morning, we have a range of snacks available today from our refreshment trolley, including hot and cold drinks, chocolate bars and pastries. My colleague is working their way along the train and is currently located in coach E at the rear.'

This was one of the most welcomed announcements I had heard and I reached into my pocket to pull out my purse in anticipation. A few more stations whizzed by and soon the refreshment trolley was next to me.

I placed my standard order – a latte – and handed over my reusable cup. The attendant pushed a button on the machine in front of him and held my container underneath. For a few seconds we both watched as the liquid filled to the top, politely smiling at one another whenever we awkwardly caught eye contact.

'Here you go, ma'am. That will be £3 please.'

I tapped my card on the contactless panel and took my drink.

'Hot or cold drinks? Snacks?' The attendant continued along the carriage, pushing the trolley in front of him and soon he had passed through the automatic doors into the next section.

I took a few sips from my cup and almost instantly I felt the caffeine begin to work and the energy levels in my body started to rise. I looked out of the window at the blurry landscapes as they flew by, trying to focus every now and then on particular objects or buildings and following them with my eyes until they escaped out of sight.

I grew bored of this game quite quickly and I wished for a pack of cards or a chess board to occupy my time. That and a worthy opponent, like my sister. For a moment I allowed the sick feelings in my stomach to return. The fear. The doubt. A few more sips of coffee were enough to suppress them. To distract myself further, I grabbed a folder from my bag and pulled out a grey ring bound notepad containing some leaflets. Being a newbie in Spiral Bay, some of the team had very kindly put together a collection of flyers to various attractions that they insisted I would need to visit before I could call myself a local. There was an array of activities on offer – sand sculpting, kayaking along the coastline, a few museums, an aquarium. The list went on.

They had also compiled a table of the best restaurants in town, including their recommended takeaways near to my new house, all ranked with scores. I found it really considerate that they were trying to make me feel like one of them, a part of the town. I scanned the takeaways in search of one that might be able to provide me with dinner this evening.

Being outside of London I had to get used to the fact that not everywhere is open all the hours under the sun. I would have to plan my life a bit more here. Since I was moving to the seaside, it seemed appropriate that my first meal should be fish and chips from the shop only a five-minute walk from my house. That would be my treat for the move, the new job and for taking a chance on a new life.

I continued to pass the time by writing up a to-do list of the places I wanted to cover across the town, all ordered from the attractions I definitely wanted to go to, down to those that I would happily visit to pass a lonely afternoon, but I wouldn't be upset to pass on. By the time I had finished I had built quite an extensive outline of my first six months, although secretly I was hoping that I would have to rain check on some of these in favour of plans with new friends.

When I eventually glanced down at my train app to check our progress, I was excited to see that we were now only five minutes from my stop. I stood up and pulled my bag out from the overhead compartment and placed it on the seat. I noticed a few other people in the carriage were also preparing to leave. I found it reassuring to think that I wasn't the only person exiting here, as if the other passengers gave the place credibility. By the time I had walked to the nearest door, the train had stopped at the station.

Stepping down onto the platform was like leaping across an invisible line that divided my old life from my new. My first impressions were good – the station looked clean and well maintained. The paintwork looked as though it had recently been updated. There were flowers lining the railings either side of the main ticket office, all vibrant colours in full bloom. I scrambled in my pocket as I walked towards the exit, readying my ticket for inspection.

'Thank you, ma'am.'

The guard standing next to the open barrier took my ticket from me as I passed by her and onto the pavement just outside the main entrance. My new house was a twenty-minute walk from the station and for a moment I considered making the journey on foot, taking the opportunity to breathe in the sea air. I quickly changed my mind when I spotted a taxi pulling into the rank opposite. There would be plenty of time for walking later, but today I had to focus on getting the house sorted.

I hopped in the backseat and told the driver the address, which I had to read from the back of my diary. I'll need to get used to my new road name. I fear that without the diary to prompt me there would be every chance I'd switch to autopilot and give the road to my old flat. Yes, I think it'll take some time before I call this place "home".

The roads we drove down were so picturesque. Everyone obviously cared about the appearance of their homes. Although mine was rented, I took an oath in that moment to make sure I maintained my front garden to the same high standards. I wonder how long it will take me to break that!

Once we had pulled alongside my driveway, I handed the driver his money, waving away the change as a tip and stepped out of the car. As he drove away, I remained there for a moment, looking up at the building in front of me, taking some time to soak everything in. The sky was a bright blue, the sun was shining down on my face and for a moment, I felt as though I was exactly where I should be.

When I pushed open the door, there were a few envelopes on the stripy blue "Welcome" mat waiting to be collected. As I rifled through the bundle, I found that most of them belonged to the previous tenant, so I placed them in a pile on a side table in the hall, ready for me to send on to the landlord at some point.

The front room was full of boxes, all stacked neatly with their labels proudly displayed on the side. Unpacking was never going to be an enjoyable task, particularly alone, so I had tried to reduce the legwork as much as possible by clearly identifying the contents of each box. I had even printed out a list, all colour coded against markings I had placed in the corner of each container. Even so, as I stood there looking at the towers of cardboard, I let a tired, undermotivated sigh escape between my lips. With my hands digging firmly into my hips, I was the picture of someone lost and frightened, standing amongst a jungle of life fragments; items I had collected throughout my thirty-five years on this earth.

I could feel my mind sinking in a quicksand of nostalgia, weighted down by an overwhelming longing for the familiar. I wanted to see Chester. He was my bridge between the old and the new. I decided that before unpacking anything, my priority should be to collect Chester from Rachel's house next door. I checked my watch: 08:30. That seemed a little early to knock on someone's door. Particularly on a Sunday. Was it too early? Perhaps Rachel worked at the weekend. Perhaps she had seen me arrive and was stood there, in her work clothes, waiting for me to go over and relieve her of my pet so she could get to her place of business on time. Or perhaps she was still asleep, with Chester curled in a ball at the foot of her bed, like he would always do back at my London flat.

I hesitated for a second, considering the potential faux pas of waking up my new neighbour. It didn't take too long to convince myself. The thought of seeing Chester again for the first time in a week was the boost I needed and so I picked my keys up from the table on my way out of the front room.

I had just turned the handle to the front door, eager to step outside, when I felt the vibrations of my mobile phone against my thigh. Frustrated, I closed the door once more and slid the phone out of my pocket to look at the number on the screen. The call was from a mobile I didn't recognise, so I cleared my throat and answered with what I considered to be my poshest phone voice.

'Kate Melrose.'

'Hello, DCI Melrose. This is DS Jack Stanford. I know your official start date is tomorrow, but we need you right away please. There's been a murder.'

3

DCI Melrose pulled into the car park of the Museum of Natural History at 9:30 a.m., stopping temporarily to show her badge to the uniformed officer stationed on the perimeter, before continuing to a parking space next to a crumbling stone wall. By the time she had stepped out of her vehicle and closed the door, a man in his early 30s had walked over to meet her.

'Good morning, ma'am.'

'Lovely to see you again, DS Stanford.' Kate reached out and shook his hand. 'Please, though, call me DCI Melrose. Ma'am makes me feel old.'

DS Stanford chuckled. 'Of course, DCI Melrose. I'm sorry we've had to call you in a day earlier, I hope you didn't have anything interesting planned today.'

'Unpacking boxes, mostly. Nothing that can't wait.'

'How are you settling in?'

'Haven't really had the chance to. Arrived on the first train out of London this morning and had only been inside the house for ten minutes or so before I received your call. Still, I guess I had to meet the locals at some point.'

DCI Melrose gestured with her head in the direction of a group of people now beginning to gather by the blue and white police tape sealing off the main entrance to the museum.

'Ah, yes. Word spreads quickly in a town like this. And it's not often we have a murder on our doorstep. Normally, we're dealing with drunk and disorderly behaviour or the occasional drugs bust. Oh, and the museum has been the victim of several burglaries in recent weeks. But, a murder? This is big news for them.'

'There was me thinking they were here to welcome me,' DCI Melrose laughed.

'Oh, I imagine that is part of the attraction as well. You've already gained celebrity status around town. As I say, word travels fast.'

DCI Melrose smiled briefly, before steering the conversation back to the matter at hand. 'What do we know so far?'

DS Stanford pulled out a notebook from his inside jacket pocket and flipped a few pages over.

'The victim is Professor Malcolm Hail, 44 years old, Head of Palaeontology here at the Museum.' He paused to look over at DCI Melrose, who was searching her pockets. 'Do you need a pad and pen?'

'This is incredibly embarrassing. I always keep my notebooks in my work jacket, which is still in a box at home. When I received your call I pretty much jumped straight in the car. Would you mind if I borrowed one, please?'

'Consider it a welcome gift,' DS Stanford joked, as he handed over a spare set.

'Thank you.'

He waited for a few more seconds to allow his colleague enough time to jot down the details he had provided so far. When she had finished, they both began walking towards the entrance of the museum.

'Who found the body?'

'The security guard, Max Roberts, discovered the body at 6 a.m., at which point he called 999. Our officers arrived on the scene around 06:15 and secured the perimeter. Dr Albert Shaftesbury, one of the medical examiners for our patch, is currently with the body. Fragments of a vase were found upstairs on the balcony, where we believe the victim fell. His office is in a bit of a mess too.'

'Perhaps he stumbled across a burglary in progress then?'

DS Stanford nodded. 'It's definitely possible.'

'And the victim's family?'

'Liaison officers are currently contacting them as we speak.'

'Thank you. I think it's probably time we take a look inside, don't you?'

'I should warn you, it's not a nice sight in there.'

'Thank you for the heads up, DS Stanford. Shall we?'

As the detectives began to walk up the steps towards the entrance, they passed the group of locals huddled inquisitively on the edge of the cordon. A few of them were jostling for a better viewing position, others were recording the action on their mobiles, eager to upload the footage to their social media pages. The bolder members of the bystanders began calling out.

'Do you know who did this?'

'Why was he killed?'

'Detective, how about a quote for our readers about this tragic incident?'

DCI Melrose stopped and turned around on the steps, preparing to address the onlookers.

'We are still in the early stages of our

investigation. When we have more information, a formal statement will be released. In the meantime, please direct all your queries to our Communications Officer, thank you.'

With that, they continued their journey up to the main door and stepped inside the entrance hall. They were met by a uniformed officer, who checked their identification before collecting some items from the table behind him.

'Please sign in here and put these on.'

The officer handed DCI Melrose a clipboard, along with protective overalls, a pair of disposable gloves and shoe covers. Kate scrawled her name and entry time on the page and handed it to DS Stanford, who did the same, before passing it back to the officer.

Photographs were being taken throughout the hall and up on the first-floor balcony. Numbered yellow markers had been left in various places across the floor. Towards the middle of the room, DCI Melrose could see the large figure of the triceratops. Impaled upon one of the horns, was the lifeless body of Professor Hail. The area surrounding the victim had been sectioned off with barriers and tape. Standing on a set of steps examining the corpse was a middle-aged man in a full protective suit. On the ground, a pool of blood had formed, which could be traced up along the dinosaur bones to where the victim was suspended.

'I presume that is Dr Shaftesbury?'

'Yes, that's him.'

'Let's have a chat with him then, find out what he has found so far. After that we need to have a talk with the security guard. Was anyone else onsite at the time the body was discovered?'

'Two other members of staff arrived just after Max

put in the call – Edith Chapman, the Museum Director and Georgie Westbrook, the Collections Co-ordinator. All three are currently in Edith's office just over there, being looked after by one of the officers. I've told them to stay there until we've had a chance to speak with them all.'

'Thank you, DS Stanford. I can see that a lot of progress has already been made.'

The detectives began heading over to where the doctor was stood. DCI Melrose scribbled a rough blueprint of the downstairs floor plan on her notepad as they walked. She stopped just before they reached the body and looked up towards the first-floor balcony. With an outstretched finger, she traced an imaginary line down to the professor's resting place. Realising that he was walking alone, DS Stanford paused to look back towards his senior colleague.

'Everything OK, DCI Melrose?'

'Just getting my bearings. Understanding the lay of the land, so to speak. That's quite a distance to fall. The impact would have been at some speed. I'm assuming this dinosaur is a model? A replica?'

'That's correct. I spoke with the museum director and this is a full sized, reinforced replica.'

'Reinforced?'

'Yes, because of its position in the main hall it has been built to withstand the unwanted contact of any curious visitors. If a child, or adult for that matter, happened to try climbing this and a piece of bone broke away, it wouldn't be good for the museum's PR.'

'I can't help but think a murder won't be either.'

Up close, DCI Melrose could see that the horn of the triceratops had gone straight through the professor's upper body. If he hadn't been dead when he fell, death wouldn't have been too far away following impact, she thought.

The medical examiner had been so engrossed in his assessment of the body that he hadn't noticed the arrival of the two detectives until he bent down to retrieve an item from his medical bag.

'Hello again, DS Stanford.' The doctor paused when he noticed Kate. 'And good morning and welcome to DCI Melrose, I presume?'

'Hello, Doctor, it's a pleasure to meet you…although, I wish our first meeting had been under slightly more light-hearted circumstances.'

The doctor nodded in acknowledgement and continued to look at the body.

'Would you mind telling us what you've found so far?' DCI Melrose asked.

'Of course.'

The doctor turned off the small headlight around his forehead and took a few steps down the ladder, to continue the conversation from a more comfortable position.

'There are a few obvious observations – the professor fell from the first-floor balcony and upon impact with the triceratops head, his body was impaled. From the initial contact, the bone shattered his spine, before piercing the heart on its way through. One of his lungs has been punctured as well. Judging from the pool of blood, he would have bled out quickly, if he wasn't already dead by then.'

DCI Melrose finished her notes and paused to look back up to the balcony.

'And there's no way he could have simply lost balance, perhaps, and just fallen over the rail?'

'There are signs of blunt force trauma – one on the back of the head and the other on the neck, which suggest he was hit, at least twice, from behind with an object.'

'The vase?' said DS Stanford.

'It's almost certain,' agreed Dr Shaftesbury. 'I found fragments of the vase in his hair. As always, we'll need to confirm all these theories at the autopsy, but based on the markings and lack of defensive wounds, it's unlikely he saw his attacker. I believe he was caught by surprise and then either fell as a result of the blow to his head, or was pushed over the balcony.'

'Do we have an estimated time of death yet, Doctor?' said DCI Melrose.

'Due to the damage caused to the body it's difficult to say for sure, but based on initial temperature readings, I would say the window we're currently looking at would be between 2 a.m. and 3 a.m. This is also backed up by his watch, which was smashed in the fall.'

'Thank you, we'll let you get on.' DCI Melrose nodded to Dr Shaftesbury, who climbed back up the steps to the body. 'So, DS Stanford, we have a 3 hour or so window where the victim lay here undiscovered.'

'Why would the night guard wait 3 hours to call the police? Surely, he would have heard or seen something.'

'My thoughts exactly. Looks like we have some questions for Mr Roberts. Either he is incredibly bad at his job…'

'Or he's involved.'

4

'I can't believe this is happening,' Edith said, as she paced up and down her office.

Georgie was sat on the edge of a beige two-seater sofa staring down at the floor. Max stood with his arms crossed behind his back, staring out of the window at the crowd that was beginning to gather near the main entrance to the museum. The police were trying to contain the onlookers as best as possible as they all shuffled strategically to try and move themselves as close as they could to the crime scene tape.

When the office door suddenly opened, the three occupants of the room quickly turned to see who the visitor was. A young-looking policewoman entered, carrying a tray of tea and biscuits, which she placed on a small table near the sofa.

'I've brought you all some refreshments. Make sure you have something to drink and eat. If there's anything else I can get you, I'll be just outside the door. The Detective Chief Inspector is on her way. Once she's reviewed the scene, she'll want to talk to you all. I'm sure it won't be too long now.'

They all nodded politely and thanked the officer as she backed out of the room and took up her sentry position outside, leaving the office door open.

'Poor Malcolm', Georgie remarked, as she leant

over to pick up a cup of tea from the tray.

'I knew I shouldn't have let him work late last night, not with all the break-ins recently,' Edith said as she walked across the room to join Georgie on the sofa, collecting a chocolate biscuit on her way past the table.

Through the window, Max could see DS Stanford in the car park talking to a woman in her mid-30s. She was making notes on her pad as the Detective Sergeant spoke and her light brown hair kept trying to break free from her loose pony tail with each gust of wind. After a few moments they made their way around to the main entrance and disappeared out of sight.

'Looks like the lead detective has arrived,' Max sighed and rubbed his forehead. 'I'm going to have a lot of explaining to do.'

'Just tell them what you told us, Max.' Edith began to walk up and down the room once more. 'What's important right now is finding whoever did this to Malcolm. And the rest...well, we can deal with that later.'

Edith was trying to maintain her composure, her professionalism. She was the most senior person in the museum and felt it was important to portray as strong an exterior as possible, even if she was crumbling inside. She wasn't a selfish person, but she couldn't help wondering how this would affect the museum. For a split second she allowed her mind to entertain the dark notion that perhaps it would be good for business – the attraction of the macabre. She dismissed this quickly with a shake of the head before walking behind her desk to sit down, full of self-judgement for even considering the thought.

'Tomorrow was supposed to be the public opening

of “Finding Fossils”,’ Georgie said timidly, as she looked up from the untouched cup of tea she had been cradling in her hands. ‘And there’s another delivery of artefacts arriving later this week, ready for the Egyptian exhibition that will take its place.’

Georgie’s grip loosened and she watched as the cup of tea fell from her hand, almost in slow motion like a scene from a movie. The brown liquid sprayed across the floor as the ceramic shattered into several pieces.

‘Is everything OK in here?’ The disturbance had alerted the police officer, who was now stood in the doorway.

‘Yes, fine thank you,’ said Edith as she rushed over to Georgie. ‘Nothing a quick clean up won’t fix.’

The officer stepped back outside. Edith sat down next to Georgie and put her arm around her.

‘We’re all in shock, Georgie, but you must remember that we’re all in this together and we’ll look out for each other, OK? Don’t think about work today. Let’s just get through the next few hours. Tomorrow we can work out what needs to be done with the museum.’

Georgie nodded as she wiped away the tears that had trickled down her cheeks. ‘You’re right, I’m sorry. I feel awful for even thinking about work. Thanks, Edith.’ Georgie managed to raise a smile, before turning to face the night guard. ‘How are you holding up, Max? You know we don’t blame you, right?’

Georgie’s softly spoken voice managed to break Max from his trance and he twisted his head slightly to glance over towards the sofa.

‘That’s kind of you to say, Georgie, but we all know I messed up. And I’ll never forgive myself for as long as I live.'

As Max shifted his attention back to the outside world, the two women looked at each other. They knew there was nothing they could say that would make a difference. They couldn't reverse time and bring Malcolm back from the dead. Nor could they lessen the guilt that Max was feeling.

For the next few minutes, the atmosphere in the room remained tense. Edith returned to the chair behind her desk and pretended to read some paperwork. Georgie stayed on the sofa, staring at the blank wall opposite. Max maintained his position by the window.

All three were trying to find comfort in their thoughts. Silence had captured the room, as they nervously awaited the arrival of DCI Melrose.

5

'Good morning, everyone. My name is Detective Chief Inspector Kate Melrose and I believe you've already met Detective Sergeant Jack Stanford.'

Kate stood in the open doorway to Edith's office, her tall, slim body carving through the light that poured in from the entrance hall. Her colleague, who matched her in height, looked on from over her right shoulder. Kate stepped inside the room, taking her notebook from her pocket.

'I understand that this is a difficult time for you, losing one of your own in these circumstances, but we will need to ask you all some questions individually, do you understand?'

The three nodded, but remained silent.

'Is there a room we can use with more privacy please?' DS Stanford asked as he stepped inside next to DCI Melrose.

'Um, yes, yes, of course,' Edith stammered slightly. She had never been interviewed by the police before and the thought of it made her nervous. 'There's a small meeting room, just the other side of the entrance to the exhibition next door. You can use that.'

'Thank you, that would be perfect. We'll begin with Mrs Chapman first, please.' DCI Melrose gestured with her arm towards the door and the three of them exited the room, leaving Max and Georgie looking at one another.

DS Stanford flicked the light switch outside the meeting room before entering. This also prompted the air conditioning unit in the ceiling to start whirring, as it began to wake from hibernation. In the middle of the room was a round table, surrounded by six chairs. The detectives claimed the two seats furthest from the door, leaving Edith to sit down opposite them both.

'I appreciate your mind must be all over the place at the moment, but DS Stanford and I need to gather as much information as possible. Anything you can think of, big or small, may help this investigation, so please do not omit any details that you feel would be relevant to the case.'

Edith forced a smile as she nodded her head gently.

'Can you start by taking us through the events of last night please, up until the point you last saw Professor Hail?'

'Of course. We were launching our new exhibition, "Finding Fossils". Malcolm was the keynote speaker and we had invited around 50 local people – prominent businesses, donors and so on, plus a few journalists. We have been working with several other museums across the world to bring this together. The exhibition was going to open here, then go on a tour.'

'We'll need a list of everyone on the guest list, please, plus any staff on duty yesterday,' interjected DCI Melrose.

'Absolutely, I can email you across the names as soon as we're done here.'

'Did anything unusual happen during the course of the evening?' said DS Stanford.

‘Well, during Malcolm’s speech, we had a late and rather rude arrival – Professor Arthur Stone. He used to work here, three years ago…before Malcolm replaced him. Professor Stone now lectures in the Department of Archaeology at the local university. I think it’s fair to say he has a bit of history with Malcolm.’

‘Was Professor Stone replaced because he had found another job, or…?’ DS Stanford left the question hanging open.

‘He was pushed out. The board wanted to freshen things up. Professor Stone was quite old fashioned, whereas Malcolm was more progressive. He understood that the museum was a business. Arthur just wanted to stay in his office. He didn’t think it was his role to interact with visitors, or get involved in any activities to help boost local interest. When Malcolm took over, he reached out to the local schools and has built a lot of key relationships with businesses too.’

‘Why was Professor Stone invited if there was bad blood between them?’ said DCI Melrose.

‘Despite their differences, Professor Stone is still an influential figure in the academic world. It didn’t seem right to leave him off the guest list. Besides, Malcolm and I agreed that as long as Arthur behaved himself, then there was no reason for him not to attend.’

‘How did Professor Hail react to Professor Stone arriving late?’ DS Stanford leaned forward and placed his hands on the table, interlocking them at the fingers.

‘Like a professional. He let it slide. I think a small part of him felt sorry for Arthur.’

‘Sorry for him? Why?’

'Professor Hail was about to be published. He was successful. Arthur's career seemed to be coming to an end. I also understand that the book was going to disprove and discredit one of Professor Stone's papers. That would have been the final nail in the coffin for him, I think.'

DCI Melrose and DS Stanford paused for a brief second and looked at one another, before they continued writing in their pads again.

'What time did Professor Stone leave the museum?' said DS Stanford.

'I don't know. I saw him at the speech, but I didn't notice him go into the exhibition. Now I think about it, I'm not sure he even did. The ribbon was cut and then there was a rush of people. Once I had gone inside with everyone else, I didn't see Professor Stone again for the rest of the evening.'

'What time did you leave the museum last night, Mrs Chapman?'

'I think it was around ten o'clock. I saw Malcolm on my way out. He said he had some news but that he would tell me about it later. I said goodnight, then left through the main door. I didn't see him again after that.'

'Do you know what he might have wanted to tell you?' said DCI Melrose.

'I thought it might be related to the recent break-ins.'

The detectives stopped writing and looked at Edith.

'Can you tell us a bit more about them, please?' DCI Melrose tilted her head forward slightly, hopeful of a response that might lead to a possible suspect.

'For the past few weeks, there have been burglaries at night and we've had items stolen from the museum. We had police officers out each time and we've been dealing with one of the other detectives from the burglary team.'

'Thank you, Mrs Chapman, we'll liaise with them back at the station. Is there anything else that you can remember at this moment in time that may help us?'

'I, er...I think that's everything, for now,' Edith stuttered slightly as she searched her mind.

'You said that you left the museum and didn't see Professor Hail after that time,' said DS Stanford. 'Can I ask where you were between 10 p.m. and 3 a.m. this morning?'

'I…I went home. I waited outside for a taxi for about 15 minutes, he arrived around 10:15 p.m. and took me straight home,' replied Edith.

'Thank you for your time,' said DCI Melrose, as she stood up and reached across the table to shake Edith's hand. 'DS Stanford will give you a contact card. Please get in touch if you think of anything else. You're free to go home now, but can you send Miss Westbrook through on your way out please?'

Edith nodded as Jack reached into his pocket and handed over a small business card, which she took before quickly leaving the room, closing the door behind her.

'So,' said DS Stanford, as he flicked back through his notes, 'a rival Professor or a bungled burglary.'

'Yes, it seems that way so far, doesn't it? Two strong leads to look into once we're done here. I wonder what Miss Westbrook and Mr Roberts will bring to the table. We'll need to check out the taxi journey as well.'

'That shouldn't be too hard,' laughed DS Stanford. 'There are only two taxi companies in the whole town!'

Their conversation was interrupted by a gentle knocking.

'Come in,' ordered DCI Melrose.

Georgie opened the door and stepped inside the small room. The skin around her eyes was puffed up and her loose, blonde hair was gathered together, hanging down just over her right shoulder.

'Please sit down, Miss Westbrook,' said DCI Melrose, as she gestured to the chair opposite. 'This is just an informal discussion about the events last night. I can see that you're understandably upset, so we won't keep you here any longer than is necessary.'

Georgie nodded and sat down.

'Miss Westbrook, can you tell us a bit about what happened at the exhibition opening yesterday please?' asked DS Stanford.

'Yes, of course. Um, well, let's see…Malcolm gave the keynote speech and opened the exhibition. We had a small group there; we always do with new exhibitions. If you give them enough champagne, they'll help spread the word. You know, "I scratch your back" and all that. It's good publicity.'

'Did anything unusual happen during the event?' questioned DCI Melrose.

'Not that I can recall…actually, yes…Professor Stone arrived bang in the middle of Malcolm's speech. He walked in late and just sat there, staring. I'm pretty sure he didn't even move when we all walked through to the exhibition. When I came back out about thirty minutes later, he had gone, but I don't recall seeing him inside Finding Fossils, so he must have left the museum shortly after the speech.'

'Was there any rivalry between Professor Stone and Professor Hail?' asked DCI Melrose.

Georgie scoffed and suppressed a slight laugh.

'Yes, you could say that. Malcolm replaced him. And to rub salt further into the wounds, he was about to publish a book that would have torn Professor Stone's career to shreds.'

'How well do you know Professor Stone?' DS Stanford shuffled slightly in his chair as he spoke, trying to find a more comfortable sitting position.

'Not very well at all. I'm aware of his reputation here and I've met him once or twice, but I've only been working at the museum for 18 months, so he was gone before I joined.'

'Can you confirm where you were between leaving the museum last night and 3 a.m. this morning, please?' said DS Stanford.

'I left the exhibition around 8 p.m. as I had dinner reservations with some friends at Rosa's, the Italian restaurant. After that I went home.'

'Can you remember the time you left the restaurant and arrived home?' asked DS Stanford.

'Erm, probably just before 1 a.m. I walked home since my flat isn't that far from the restaurant.'

'Thank you, Miss Westbrook,' said DCI Melrose. 'Just a few more questions and then you'll be able to go home. Is there anything else you can think of that might help with our investigation?'

'Well, I'm sure it's nothing, but, um, yes, well, I was walking past Malcolm's office last week and I heard him in an argument on the phone.'

'Do you know what the argument was about or the identity of the caller?' asked DS Stanford.

'The door was shut, so I could only pick out a few words here and there, but I'm sure I heard him say, "stalker" and "Alice".'

'And Alice is…?' said DCI Melrose.

'His ex-wife. They divorced about a year ago.'

'Do you know what Professor Hail meant by "stalker"?' said DS Stanford. 'Had he mentioned being stalked to you?'

Georgie shook her head. 'No, I don't know who he was referring to, sorry.'

'Thank you, Miss Westbrook, I think that's probably all we need from you for now.' DCI Melrose walked over to the door and opened it. 'Please send in Mr Roberts on your way out.'

Georgie stood up and pushed the chair back under the table before walking towards the exit. As she passed DCI Melrose, she paused and turned back.

'Detectives, do you think this is an isolated incident or could other people at the museum also be a target? I just want to make sure it's safe here. We often work alone late into the evening in our offices.'

'We're still in the very early stages of the investigation, but there's nothing at present to suggest a wider threat,' said DCI Melrose. 'If that changes, we'll be in touch.'

Once Georgie had moved out of sight, Kate closed the door and turned to Jack, who was still making notes.

'I'm guessing we need to add the ex-wife to our list of possible suspects?' said DS Stanford, as he looked up from his pad.

'So, we've got break-ins, an angry Professor and a stalker ex-wife,' summarised DCI Melrose. 'I guess three leads is better than none. I wonder if we'll get a fourth suspect from our night guard, assuming that we can discount him as one after we've had our chat. Once we're finished here, I want to take a look at the first-floor balcony where he fell. And also, his office. After that, we'll head back to the station.'

'Sounds good,' agreed DS Stanford, just as there

was a double knock at the door.

DCI Melrose walked to her chair and sat down, before acknowledging their visitor. The sunken frame of the sixty-year-old guard shuffled in, his silver hair poking out from beneath his cap.

'Please take a seat, Mr Roberts,' said DS Stanford. 'Perhaps we could start with where you were when Professor Hail was murdered and the time that followed, up until the point you discovered the body.'

Max looked down at his crumpled hands. He felt as though his entire body was sweating and every muscle seemed to ache.

'Mr Roberts?' prompted DCI Melrose.

'Asleep,' whispered Max, ashamed to let the word leave his lips.

'I'm sorry, can you repeat that and speak louder please, Mr Roberts?' ordered DS Stanford.

'I was asleep!' shouted Max.

The room fell silent for a few moments. The two detectives glanced at one another, before turning back to look across the table at the weeping man in front of them.

'I'm a fucking night guard and I was asleep,' sobbed Max, his hands shaking and saliva falling from his open mouth as he cried. 'Professor Hail died because I wasn't doing my fucking job!'

'Mr Roberts, sit back and take a deep breath please,' said DCI Melrose. 'Try to calm yourself down.'

DS Stanford slid a packet of tissues towards Max. The guard struggled to open the plastic wrapping as his hands were shaking, so the Detective Sergeant removed a tissue for him and handed it over.

'Thank you,' Max sighed. 'I'm sorry. I'm really sorry.'

'That's OK, Mr Roberts. We understand this is a difficult time. We're just trying to establish the facts,' said DS Stanford. 'Perhaps it would help if you took us through your shift, please, from when you arrived until you found the body. Did anything unusual happen? Did you see anything out of the ordinary?'

'I, er, began my shift at 7 p.m. last night. There were still people here from the exhibition, but by about half nine most people had gone. Edith was the last person to leave the building, as Malcolm was walking up to his office. About ten minutes later, I started one of the first patrols of the night. When I was passing the Professor's office, I heard a banging noise so I stopped to check everything was OK.'

'What did you see?' asked DCI Melrose.

'The professor was searching for something, most of his office had been turned over. Then when he saw me in the doorway he asked if anyone had been in his office. Something had been stolen, you see.'

'Another break-in?' said DS Stanford.

'No, I don't think so. There was something different about this one. It was almost as if he knew who was behind the theft. I asked if he wanted me to call the police and he said that he would deal with it himself. He was pretty worked up, so I decided it would be best to leave him to it. I think he might have had a bit too much to drink. I carried on my patrol and then returned to my office at the front of the museum.'

'What time did you fall asleep?' said DS Stanford.

'It would have been close to midnight, I guess.'

'And you slept through until early this morning, when you found the body? You didn't wake in between, or hear anything else?' questioned DCI Melrose.

‘I was asleep the whole time. Look, I’ve been picking up extra shifts recently. I need the money. But the shift patterns have taken a toll on me. I woke up just before 6 a.m., made a cup of tea and then went to start opening up the rooms. That’s when I saw Professor Hail impaled on the dinosaur bones. I’d never seen anything like it in my life. I had to run to the toilet to be sick. After that I called 999.’

‘Mr Roberts,’ said DCI Melrose. ‘Do you have any evidence to prove that you were asleep during this time?’

‘No…well, possibly. The only thing I can think of is the CCTV camera in the corner of the security office. That might show me asleep on the couch.’

‘Might?’ said DS Stanford.

‘Well, they’re pretty crap cameras.’

‘Are there other cameras throughout the museum? Is it possible that our attacker might have been caught on one of them?’ asked DS Stanford.

Max shrugged. ‘It’s possible, but like I said, they’re not the best cameras, so the image might be a bit blurry.’

‘Where are the recordings stored?’

‘We have a hard drive in the office and they’re also backed up offsite by our security company.’

‘We’ll need access to the hard drive,’ said DCI Melrose. ‘Is there anything else you can tell us that might help with our investigation? You said this was different to the previous break-ins, what makes you think that?’

‘In the other break-ins they didn’t bother going to the offices, they were stealing artefacts.’

‘And there’s no footage of anyone carrying out the burglaries on the CCTV?’ said DS Stanford.

‘Whoever is behind the break-ins knows the layout

of the museum; they know exactly where the cameras and the blind spots are. I doubt there's anything on the footage that would help identify who the thief is. Like I said, the CCTV in the museum is older than most of the items on display. It's laughable really.'

'OK, Mr Roberts, thank you for your time,' said DCI Melrose.

'I'm free to go?' checked the night guard.

'For now, yes. We may have some more questions for you later though,' said DCI Melrose.

'OK, thank you. Your officer has my address. And if I'm not there, I'm probably at my allotment, just off Bay View Road.'

Max quickly vacated his seat and headed for the door. For a few seconds his hands fumbled nervously at the handle, as if he was struggling to grip the metal surface in his haste. Eventually, he succeeded and exited the room, closing the door behind him.

'What do you think, DCI Melrose?'

'Let's get the copies of the cameras and have them checked over back at the station. We should liaise with the team looking into the burglaries as well. For all we know, there may be a connection. We also shouldn't rule out the possibility of a stalker, so it would be a good idea to interview the ex-wife tomorrow and catch up with Professor Stone as well. But for now, let's take a look upstairs. Perhaps we'll find some more answers there.'

6

DCI Melrose and DS Stanford climbed to the top of the main staircase and began to walk along the partially carpeted first-floor balcony. Several numbered yellow markers had been placed across the floor, each pinpointing a potential piece of evidence. Photographs were still being taken, as the SOCOs continued their search for further items of interest.

The detectives reached the area that had been identified as the location of the attack. Tape had been used to mark the section from which Professor Hail had fallen to his death. Scattered across the floor were the broken shards of the vase. Some of the pieces had blood stains on them. DCI Melrose stepped towards the wooden rail and leant over to look down at the hall below.

'This is quite a height,' she said, gripping on firmly. 'Even with a soft landing, I don't think anyone would survive a fall from up here.'

'Do you think the killer had intended for the victim to end up on the triceratops model?' said DS Stanford.

'It's possible, but unlikely. Look over there,' said DCI Melrose, pointing towards an empty display stand. 'That seems to be where the vase was taken from, which suggests the attack was opportunistic. Perhaps Professor Hail had stumbled upon an intruder and they struck him with the object closest to them.'

'Based on Dr Shaftesbury's measurements, the victim was a similar height to me,' said DS Stanford. 'If I stand up against the barrier, the top of the rail sits just above my waist. Maybe the professor heard a noise in the hall below and was leaning over when the attacker struck him from behind. With the way his weight was distributed, it wouldn't have taken much effort for him to go over.'

'That would certainly make sense,' agreed DCI Melrose. 'But it also makes it harder to determine an approximate height of our attacker.'

They were interrupted by the arrival of Dr Shaftesbury, who had discretely appeared behind them. He took a navy handkerchief from his back pocket and mopped the sweat from his brow.

'I'm signing the body over now, ready to be taken back for the post-mortem,' he informed the detectives. 'Is there anything else you need to ask me before I go?'

'Actually, yes,' said DCI Melrose. 'Did you find any evidence on the body that would suggest he was helped over this ledge? I mean, besides the blunt force trauma on the head?'

'Yes, there were some rips in the back of his trousers. I also found pressure marks and bruising around the ankles, which could have been caused by someone grabbing them tightly.'

'So, they could have hit the victim from behind, then when he fell forward onto the balcony bar, grabbed him by the ankles to pivot him over?' asked DS Stanford.

'That would be consistent with what I've found so far, yes,' confirmed Dr Shaftesbury. 'But I wouldn't be able to say for definite until results are back from the post-mortem. If there's nothing else?'

'No, that's all for now, thank you for your help,' said DCI Melrose, unaware that the medical examiner had already begun to walk back towards the stairs.

'Don't worry, he's like that with everyone – all business,' laughed DS Stanford. 'But he is the best of the best. Even if he is about as warm as the bodies he examines.'

DCI Melrose smiled. 'I don't think there's anything more out here that can help us. Let's go and take a look around the office.'

They walked away from the balcony and through a doorway that led to a dimly-lit, narrow corridor. As they approached the door to the Professor's office, they could see that two members of the forensics team were still searching the room and taking photographs. Several items considered to be key pieces of evidence had been stored in a box, all marked and bagged, ready for collection. DS Stanford was about to step inside when DCI Melrose put her arm across to block him.

'I always find it helps to appreciate the bigger picture first. Just take it in,' she advised him. 'Look around. Try to imagine what might have happened here.'

For the next few moments, the detectives remained outside, surveying the interior of the room.

'Now we've had time to absorb everything, we can start breaking the room down into chunks,' said DCI Melrose, before leaning forward slightly through the open doorway. 'We OK to step in, team?'

'The room's all yours. We'll only be another five minutes or so, then we'll be out of your hair completely,' one of the investigators replied. 'Be careful of the glass on the floor over there.'

‘Thanks,’ said DCI Melrose as she crossed the threshold, followed closely by DS Stanford.

They slowly made their way towards the Professor’s desk, both continuing to scan the room from left to right, searching for any clues that may have been missed. DS Stanford headed behind the desk and picked up a glass, rotating it in the light before holding it below his nose.

‘I think it’s safe to say our victim had been drinking,’ he said, placing the glass back down and tapping on the bottle of rum.

‘Phone’s been smashed pretty bad. Looks like some of it ended up going through the bookcase over there,’ observed DCI Melrose. ‘Let’s get a record of any incoming or outgoing calls to this number since 10 p.m. last night. Mr Roberts said that when he came by here, the Professor didn’t want to phone the police about the theft because he wanted to deal with it himself. If he made a call to the person that he blamed for the theft, we should be able trace the number.’

DCI Melrose paused as she looked at a painting on the wall, leaning in closer to read the scribbled signature.

‘This is certainly an impressive painting and in a particularly nice frame too. The signature isn’t clear, but I think the surname of the painter is “Hail”. I can’t quite make out the first name, although it looks like it begins with the letter “M”.’

‘Self-portrait, perhaps?’ said DS Stanford.

‘No, I don’t think so. The first name definitely isn’t “Malcolm”. It looks more like it might be “Mark”. I’m not sure I’d want a giant painting of myself in my own office. Seems slightly pretentious.’

DS Stanford knelt down behind the desk and checked the discarded drawers and documents that were strewn across the floor. DCI Melrose walked across to the damaged bookcase, treading carefully between the shards of glass that were spread out like a minefield. She looked at the broken remains of the phone – some bits were lying on the ground; some she could see resting on the shelves through the shattered panes of glass.

'Whatever was taken, it must have made our victim pretty angry for him to cause this much destruction,' remarked DCI Melrose, turning back to look in the direction of her colleague.

'Yeah, he's definitely gone to town on this place. Although, the alcohol may have fuelled some of that rage. It reminds me of a…wait a minute.' DS Stanford paused and looked up through a gap underneath the top of the table, which had previously been occupied by a drawer. 'There's an envelope taped on the underside of this shelf. Excuse me, could you grab a shot of this please?'

One of the photographers walked over to where the detective was sat and crouched beside him, pointing the lens of their camera into the hole. The shutter clicked as the flash lit up the dim compartment. After checking the quality of the photo on the small LCD screen, they stood up and returned to their previous position.

'Thank you,' said DS Stanford, moving himself into a better position to reach inside. He placed his arm through the open space, fishing around with his gloved hand until he could feel the paper between his fingertips. With a sharp pull, he tore the package away from the wooden panel and brought it out into the open.

By the time DS Stanford was on his feet again, DCI Melrose was already waiting for him on the other side of the table. DS Stanford held the package up triumphantly.

'It has 623 written on it,' said DCI Melrose.

'623? I wonder what that means. Raffle prize, perhaps?'

The detective ran his fingers along the sticky seal at one end and tipped the contents out onto the surface of the desk. A passport with a gold crest on the front cover fell out. As DCI Melrose picked it up and flicked through the pages, a folded piece of paper dropped onto the table.

'Definitely not a raffle prize,' said DCI Melrose.

'Why would he tape his passport underneath his desk at work?' said DS Stanford, picking up the piece of paper and unfolding it. 'And why would he keep his birth certificate inside? No, wait. This isn't Professor Hail's birth certificate; it belongs to someone called…'

'William Carter?' interjected DCI Melrose.

'Yes. How did you...? But who on earth is William Carter?' asked DS Stanford.

DCI Melrose held up the passport, her fingers and thumb keeping the book open on the owner's details.

DS Stanford stared at the document in disbelief. The small, rectangular photo on the left was undeniably a picture of their victim. But the name printed alongside did not match.

'According to this, Professor Hail was also known as "William Carter",' said DCI Melrose.

7

When DCI Melrose and DS Stanford walked onto the first floor of the Spiral Bay Police Station it was already mid-afternoon and a handful of officers were in the middle of rearranging the furniture, ready for their arrival.

Several tables had been pulled into a group, all angled in the direction of a large whiteboard on wheels. In the top left corner of the board, the case number had been written along with Kate's name, as the senior investigator.

'Welcome to your new office, DCI Melrose,' smiled DS Stanford. 'This will be your investigation room. Do you want a quick tour of the station before we get started?'

'Perhaps later, if that's OK?' replied DCI Melrose, before leaning in towards DS Stanford and lowering her voice. 'Although, if you could just point me in the direction of the ladies' toilets, please? It's been a long morning!'

'Of course. It's just through that back door there. Take a right and follow the corridor down.' DS Stanford used a series of hand gestures to compliment his descriptions.

DCI Melrose nodded and exited the room. Jack took off his coat and hung it on a hook by the main office door, before walking over and sitting at one of the desks.

By the time DCI Melrose returned, many of the staff involved with the logistical arrangements of the office layout had gone, leaving only two – Detective Constable Claire Murphy and Detective Constable Joseph North. As the senior investigator made her way across the room, the DCs quickly took their places behind two of the remaining desks.

'Good afternoon DC Murphy and DC North, it's great to see you both again. Thank you for getting the ball rolling here and overseeing the room preparations. I see you've had to dig out and dust off the whiteboard.'

DCI Melrose blew along the surface, coughing as a cloud of dirt spread into the air.

'It's not often we get a murder around here, ma'am,' said DC Murphy.

'Let's hope it's not a common occurrence now that I've arrived then. I'd hate to get a bad name for myself,' replied DCI Melrose. 'And can you remind me where the evidence store is?'

'Down in the basement, boss,' said DC North.

'Thank you. Are we waiting for anyone else?' checked DCI Melrose, looking towards the main door at the back of the room.

'This is the whole team, boss. We're only a small, seaside station. You're not in London now,' quipped DC North.

DS Stanford swivelled in his chair and aimed a disgruntled stare at his junior colleague.

'I'm aware of that Detective Constable,' said DCI Melrose. 'But thank you for highlighting the obvious. Let's put those investigative skills to work with this murder, shall we?'

DS Stanford sat back in his chair, trying to conceal

a smirk. DC North had always been an arrogant smart arse, perhaps he had finally met his match in DCI Melrose, thought Jack.

'What do we know so far, ma'am?' asked DC Murphy eagerly.

DCI Melrose pulled out her notebook and removed a batch of photographs that had been obtained from the museum staffing system.

'Our victim is Professor Malcolm Hail, 44 years old, Head of Palaeontology at the museum,' said DCI Melrose. 'He may also go by the name "William Carter", according to documents we found in his office.'

'Two identities?' said DC Murphy. 'Seems a bit odd for a museum worker.'

'Maybe he's a spy,' said DC North.

'That's where we come into this,' said DCI Melrose. 'It's our job to find out.'

She lined up his photograph at the top of the board, encouraging the sticky tape to attach itself to the metallic surface by running her hand back and forth along the rectangular strip. Next to the photo she wrote: "Professor Malcolm Hail / William Carter".

'He has a blunt force trauma to the back of his head and was found impaled on the horns of a triceratops model in the main hall of the museum,' continued DCI Melrose. 'The body was discovered by this man – night guard, Max Roberts.'

She added Max's picture to the board, just below the photo of the victim.

'Mr Roberts told us that he was asleep at the time of the murder. So, here is one of our first tasks,' said DCI Melrose, moving across to the left side of the whiteboard and writing "Tasks" at the top and underlining it twice. 'There are CCTV cameras in the museum. The footage is stored onsite on a hard drive, but Mr Roberts informs us they are also backed up by the security company. Be warned though – I'm told that they aren't very good quality. Even so, we need to get copies of the footage – not only are we looking for evidence of the murder taking place, we're also looking for tape that will exonerate Mr Roberts. If he tells us he was asleep when the Professor was killed, let's find the proof.'

'Not much of a night guard then,' joked DC North, breaking out into laughter.

'That'll do, Detective Constable,' said DS Stanford sternly. 'If you keep on with the wise remarks, I'll see that you're transferred straight back to burglary with DI Swift.'

The smile dropped from the young constable's face as soon as he heard those words.

'Thank you, DS Stanford,' nodded DCI Melrose. 'And thank you for volunteering for the task of going through hours of footage, DC North. Back to the briefing – this morning we also interviewed two other members of staff; both were present at the opening of the "Finding Fossils" exhibition last night. We have Edith Chapman, the Museum Director and Georgie Westbrook, Collections Co-Ordinator.'

Kate placed both their photos on the board either side of the night guard's.

'Since both Edith and Georgie had contact with our victim in the hours leading to his death, we also need to check both of their alibis. Mrs Chapman said she took a taxi home at 10:15 p.m. from the museum and Miss Westbrook went to Rosa's, an Italian restaurant in town, to meet some friends. DC Murphy, can you look into these for me, please?'

'Yes, ma'am, no problem,' replied Claire, adding

to the notes she had already been making during the briefing.

'We'll need access to the phone records for Professor Hail's landline at the museum and also his email accounts, professional and personal. Let's get access to his financials too. Since DC North has bagged himself a ticket to the movies, would you mind getting the ball rolling on that please, DC Murphy?'

'Of course, ma'am,' smiled DC Murphy, excited at the prospect of being handed extra responsibility in her first case under DCI Melrose.

'We've also been given two other people of interest. Firstly, Alice, the professor's ex-wife. Georgie Westbrook overheard the victim arguing on the phone with Alice recently. Secondly, Professor Arthur Stone, who seems to have had a professional rivalry with our victim. DS Stanford and I will look into these two. Remember to include the name "William Carter" in your searches as well. I'm going to reach out to DI Swift and ask him to brief us on the investigation into the recent break-ins at the museum to see if we can find any connection to the murder. Are there any questions?'

The two constables shook their heads, before quickly getting to work – DC Murphy turned to face her computer screen and began typing, whilst DC North picked up his phone and started to dial an outside line.

DCI Melrose proudly sat down at her fresh, new desk, which was positioned just to the right-hand side of the investigation board, facing her team.

'I know we'll have time for a proper station tour later on, but there is one room, other than the toilets, that is of great importance and I wouldn't be doing my job if I didn't show you it now,' said DS Stanford, with a seriousness to his tone. 'Would you follow me please?'

Feeling slightly confused, DCI Melrose wheeled her chair back and stood up, before walking with the Detective Sergeant across the office to a doorway in the middle of the room.

'Just inside here,' gestured Jack, opening the door.

DCI Melrose chuckled as she stepped past him and walked inside. Running along one side was a sink and worktop with a grey microwave, cream kettle, black coffee machine and some blue tins. Attached to the wall above were four cupboards and below the counter was a refrigerator. One of the doors had been labelled "Cups and Mugs", although Kate noticed that someone had lightly pencilled over this to turn the wording into "Cops and Mugshots".

On the other side of the room was a brown sofa with some cushions and next to that was a square table with four dining chairs. A small TV had been fixed to the wall opposite the door and a cork noticeboard hung beneath with various pieces of paper pinned to it.

'Tea or coffee?' said Jack, picking up the kettle and filling it with fresh water from the cold tap.

'Tea would be great, thank you,' answered Kate.

'There should be some biscuits in the middle one, if you're peckish,' said Jack, as he placed the kettle back onto its base and flicked the switch on.

Kate opened the small cupboard door and took out a plastic box, which she placed on the worktop. Inside were a variety of biscuits, some now broken into several pieces.

'This is a better setup than I've got back at home at the moment,' joked Kate. 'Perhaps I should just sleep on the sofa here tonight.'

'Well, I've spent a few nights on there myself,' confessed Jack. 'You could do a lot worse, trust me. In fact, I think I've had better sleeps on there compared to some of the hotels I've stayed in.'

This prompted a snort from DCI Melrose, who was immediately overcome with embarrassment.

'You must have stayed in some pretty seedy hotels then,' she said, before shifting the conversation. 'DC North seems an interesting one.'

'Yeah, he likes to think he's funny,' said DS Stanford. 'Sometimes he goes a bit far. But he's a good DC and he works hard. It's probably just been a while since he had a woman pulling his strings. Some men struggle with that. He'll work it out, though, don't worry.'

'I understand from his file that he only put in for a transfer to my team a few weeks ago. Any idea why? He must have known I was a woman.'

'DI Roman Swift is the reason. You'll meet him soon enough. Between you and me, he can be an absolute bastard. His approach is a bit…how can I put this politely? Questionable, shall we say? But he seems to get results so he is generally left alone by the brass.'

'I look forward to meeting him,' said DCI Melrose, partly tongue in cheek. 'But, why did DC North wait until now to transfer?'

'DI Swift had been going through the application process for a more senior role and was convinced it was in the bag for him. But when the job was given to someone else, I guess DC North thought the best thing to do would be to get out. If Swift was a bastard before, he could only get worse after a rejection like that.'

DS Stanford poured two cups of tea and handed one across to DCI Melrose. They both quickly grabbed some biscuits before returning the box to the cupboard.

'Oh, by the way, there's probably something you should know,' said DS Stanford, stirring his tea with a smile creeping across his face. 'It was your job that DI Swift applied for.'

8

I slowed the car to a stop on the gravel driveway and turned off the ignition, before slumping back into the seat and letting out a sigh. Through the gap in the steering wheel, I could see that it was just beyond half past ten.

I raised my left hand up to my face and rubbed both of my weary eyes for a few seconds. I had wanted to lead my own team for years, but I hadn't expected to walk straight into a murder inquiry a day before I had even officially started.

When I was originally offered the posting at Spiral Bay, I looked over the crime stats and had been worried that the position would not be challenging enough for me. Ha! The irony. Still, better to get stuck in and hit the ground running, I suppose.

The stones crunched beneath my feet as I stepped out of the car and walked towards my front door. I could feel a slight ache in my stomach, no doubt due to my lack of food that day. I paused outside for a moment, reflecting on how much nicer it was to arrive home from a long shift to be greeted by a house with a front garden. How much nicer it was not to have to shoulder barge a communal door open because it had swollen and stuck to the frame. The comforting thought that when I stepped inside, that was it – I was home. I didn't have another two staircases to climb or an obstacle course made up of bicycles and baskets to brave like an Olympic hurdler.

In many ways, the most treacherous part of my journey through London involved the remaining few metres once I was in my block of flats. I ended up with several sprained ankles and wrists from misjudging a leap or two (admittedly, some of those were after an evening of pub visits).

As I stepped inside, I bent down to grab a folded piece of paper that was resting on the mat and opened it to reveal a hand written message inside:

"Hi Kate, I noticed that you've been out most of the day, but I'm usually awake until at least 11 p.m. if you wanted to pop over for Chester. No worries if not. I'll be home from about 4 p.m. tomorrow evening if that would be better for you. Hope you're settling in OK, anything you need just shout. We should grab a coffee sometime. Best wishes, Rachel."

I smiled as I folded the paper back up and placed it on the side table. How nice to have someone thoughtful living next door. I peered out through a small window at the foot of the stairs in the direction of Rachel's house. Yes! There was still a light on downstairs. I wasn't going to let anything get in my way this time as I rushed outside and jogged up towards my neighbour's porch.

When I reached the front door, the brightest sensor light I had ever seen beamed down upon me, exposing me and most of the beautifully arranged flower pots beneath Rachel's bay window, almost blinding me in the process. Now I know how famous people feel when they're walking the red carpet. How do they see where they're going?

After fumbling slightly (still struggling to focus), I

was able to locate and push the doorbell.

'Hello?'

A slightly distorted voice boomed out from a small box on the wall, rushing into the night air and breaking the peaceful silence.

'Hi, Rachel? It's Kate Melrose, from next door. I'm really sorry to –'

'Kate! Hello! Stay there, I'll be right out.'

As I waited, I could feel another twinging sensation in my abdomen, but I didn't have much time to react to it. Through the decorative stained glass, I could see a figure walking down the hallway towards me. After a few clunking and clicking noises, the door flung open, revealing Rachel in her pyjamas and dressing gown.

'I'm really sorry to knock so late.'

'Don't be silly, Kate. Why don't you come in and wait on the sofa while I grab all of Chester's bits and pieces? Oh, and Chester as well of course!'

Rachel's face scrunched up as she let out a short burst of laughter. She was an attractive woman, probably around the same age as me. She encouraged me again with a wave of her hand and I stepped inside her hallway.

'Just through there.' Rachel pointed to the right as she closed the door behind me.

I passed through an open doorway into a cosy room occupied by a grey two-seater sofa, an armchair and a fire place. A TV was tucked in the corner, a few DVDs stacked next to it, mostly consisting of films and shows for children. From the amount of dust gathered on them, I suspected they hadn't been touched for a while. A narrow wooden shelf overflowing with various trinkets was hung upon the wall to my left. Beside the armchair were piles and piles of books.

'I'm more into reading than watching,' said Rachel, as if she could read my thoughts.

I smiled politely as I moved across to the sofa and sat down. Observing my surroundings had rubbed off on me from being a detective. Whether it was going into an unfamiliar place or meeting a new person, I took everything in. There have been a few awkward moments in my past where some of my friends and family have accused me of being too nosey. I guess it's not always easy to separate work and home life.

'I'll just go and get everything sorted.'

Rachel quickly scurried back into the hall and disappeared upstairs. On the mantelpiece opposite me was a picture of a young boy. I quietly walked across the room to get a closer look. The boy was sat on some large rocks by the sea, staring at the camera with a massive grin on his face. I picked the frame up and examined the photo more closely. Perhaps he was Rachel's nephew.

'My son,' said Rachel from the doorway.

Her sudden re-appearance had caught me by surprise. I found myself juggling the picture between my hands before watching in horror as it slipped from my grasp onto the tiled hearth below, shattering the glass.

'Oh, shit,' I inadvertently blurted out. 'Rachel, I'm so, so sorry. I didn't mean to…I'm sorry.'

I quickly knelt down to retrieve the broken frame.

'It's fine, don't worry about it.'

'I didn't realise you had a son,' I said, handing the broken picture across.

Rachel took it from me and sat down in the armchair, staring at the boy's face as if she was stuck in a trance. I returned to my original place on the sofa and we both sat in silence for a few moments.

'Alex,' said Rachel, breaking through the awkwardness. 'His name…was Alex.'

'What happened?' As the words left my mouth, I realised how intrusive they sounded. I barely knew Rachel and I had let my inquisitive nature get the better of me.

For a while she didn't say anything. She remained in her chair; her eyes fixed on the picture of Alex. I quickly changed the subject.

'I'm really grateful to you for helping me out with the big fluff ball. And I'm sure he'll be over to visit once I start letting him loose in the garden. I've, er…I've probably imposed on you enough for one evening. I'd better get Chester back home and I need to get some dinner.'

Rachel placed the picture down and looked up. 'At this hour?'

'I was called into work today and it's been a bit full on. Barring a few biscuits at the station, I haven't had much opportunity for food.'

'Ah, yes, the death of the professor at the museum.'

'Yes, how did you know?'

'Twitter – someone even took your picture walking in. Not much happens in this town, so when it does, it's everywhere.'

Great, I thought.

'I'll try to remember that,' I said, standing up. 'Thanks again, for everything. And I'm sorry about the photo.'

'Don't worry. Honestly. Anyway, I've put Chester's stuff in a bag by the door. He's sleeping in his travel box at the foot of the stairs.'

I walked into the hallway and scooped the bag

under my arm, leaving my other hand free to grab the handle of Chester's cage. Rachel walked ahead of me and opened the front door.

'Goodnight, Rachel.'

'Goodnight, Kate.'

I heard the door click behind me and the various locks and chains had been secured by the time I reached the end of her driveway. Back inside my house, I put the bag down in the front room and opened the cage, peering inside. Chester was curled up in a ball, fast asleep. I decided it would be unfair to wake him now, so I left him there and placed a bowl of water on the floor outside his temporary bed.

As I stood up and walked through to the kitchen, I felt another pain in my stomach. This one was more severe and sudden than the previous and I doubled over, grabbing onto the worktop to stop myself from collapsing in a heap on the floor.

Not this.

Not now.

Please.

Not again.

9

'Fuck!'

I screamed out in agony, causing Chester to jump up in his cage, rattling his poor little head against the roof. By the time he came trotting wearily into the kitchen I was already in the foetal position on the floor, cradling my stomach. He pawed at my back, rubbing his face along my jumper, letting out a miaow. He had seen this behaviour before when we lived in London and the outcome was nearly always the same.

'I'm not going back to hospital,' I said in a whisper, partly restricted by pain, partly by fear. I didn't know whether I was trying to reassure Chester or myself. I wondered how much he understood. I wondered what he had thought all the times he'd found me in a heap on the floor, rolling about in agony, tears streaming down my face.

After a few moments, I began to focus on controlling my breathing, counting in and out. I was able to move myself slowly into a kneeling position within grasping distance of my bag. I reached out and pulled it towards me, searching inside for the box of painkillers I always carry with me.

I could stand long enough to run the tap and then, realising I had not unpacked any glasses, quickly put the tablets in my mouth and lifted myself up in order to position my mouth below the flow of the water. The pain in my stomach was unbearable and it took all my mental and physical strength to stay standing long enough to swallow.

I was just able to turn off the tap, before I dropped back to the floor, crying out. I struggled to keep myself upright, resting against the cupboard door with my legs bent beneath me. I focussed on my breathing again.

In, two, three, four, hold.

Out, two, three, four.

And repeat.

In, two, three, four, hold.

Out, two, three, four.

I kept this pattern on a rotation for the next quarter of an hour as I waited for the pain to subside.

I closed my eyes, hoping this would help to calm me, but the flashbacks began. I could see the bright, blue lights of the ambulance illuminating the night sky. Even now, I still flinch at the sight of flashing lights on emergency vehicles. An unfortunate phobia to develop as a detective.

I tried to open my eyes, to bring myself back from the past, but the memories were too vivid. My mind was forcing me to face the past again. I heard the words of the paramedics as they stood beside my bed, asking me question after question.

'Miss Melrose, my name is Stephen and this is Asha. We're paramedics here to help you. Do you mind if we call you Kate?'

'When did the pain begin?'

'Can you show us with your hands where the pain is, please?'

'Have you taken any painkillers?'

Next, they inserted a cannula into my hand,

administering IV paracetamol. Following this, I was hooked up to a bag of fluids. Stephen left the room briefly, returning empty handed a few moments later, nodding to his colleague as he entered the room.

'Kate, my dear, we're going to take you to the hospital,' said Asha, gripping my hand in hers.

I whimpered, I squirmed and I tried to pool every resource I had to give me the strength to scream out, 'NO!', but by now my body and mind had given up.

'Do you think you'll be able to walk to the ambulance with us?'

I tried standing, but was overcome by the intensity of the pain and collapsed into Stephen's arms.

'Kate, the paracetamol should begin to kick in within a few minutes. We just need to get you down the stairs. There's a stretcher waiting for you at the bottom. Do you think you can walk downstairs with my support?'

I nodded.

I felt like a new-born child, learning to walk again, dragging each foot slowly beyond the other as I began my descent. Stephen was almost carrying me towards the end, with Asha following closely behind, holding the bag of fluids in the air.

As I clambered onto the stretcher, I collapsed in a tired heap. The sharp stabbing sensation in my abdomen had eased slightly, perhaps aided by the pain relief. The paramedics quickly wheeled me outside and into the back of the ambulance.

Within 15 minutes we had arrived at A&E and I was pushed into an observation cubicle, with a blue paper curtain pulled across each side. At this point, Stephen and Asha wished me well and left. I did see them again, once, on a professional level. Bizarrely, they happened to be the first responders at one of my crime scenes. Although none of us actually acknowledged our prior meeting, it reminded me how small the world really is. There aren't many places to hide. There aren't many places you can be anonymous.

I had only been waiting in the cubicle for a few moments when an Emergency Doctor in green scrubs stepped inside.

'Good evening, Miss Melrose, my name is Doctor Sullivan. Can you confirm your date of birth please?'

She then asked me to lay on my back so she could examine my stomach before I was taken for an x-ray. Various other members of the healthcare staff came and went. I had my blood taken, my cannula replaced, more fluids put up. As time went on, the paracetamol started to wear off and the pain began increasing again.

'On a scale of 1 to 10, how would you rate your pain at the moment, Miss Melrose?'

'Nine.'

'Do you have any allergies?'

'None that I know of.'

'Have you had morphine before?'

'No.'

'OK, we're going to set up a PCA with some morphine. You'll have control of a button that will allow you to administer morphine every 5 minutes, OK? It isn't clear from your x-ray what is going on, so I am admitting you to one of our gastro wards to be seen by one of their team. Lucky for you they have a bed available.'

No one came to see me that night. I had been given my own side room, with the PCA and drips by my side. I don't know if you've ever tried to sleep in a hospital at night, but you can't. Even in a side room, with the beeping of the machines around you, or the movement outside the door as the staff tend to other patients, there is so much going on. The fluorescent lights are even brighter when you're in pain and your eyes have become sensitive.

The morphine helped to bring the level of pain down to around 4. On the downside, it had also caused me to be sick, several times into the cardboard bowls. There is something very sobering about needing to push a call button to bring someone to you. Suddenly, you aren't in control anymore. You are reliant. You are at the mercy of other people.

There was a mixture of personalities on shift that night, which ranged from kind and compassionate, to cold and frustrated. Almost like a good nurse, bad nurse routine. One would come in, check how I was, ask if I needed anything; then the other would turn up complaining about being short staffed and asking me to leave the sick bowls to one side and she would collect them all later in one go.

I eventually managed to get some sleep in the early hours of the morning, but I was awoken at 8 a.m. by the consultant and his team, who were stood around my bed looking at me like an animal in a zoo.

'Good morning, Miss Melrose. My name is Doctor Ahmed, I'm the Gastroenterology Consultant here. I've been reviewing your notes – you've had quite a nasty time I can see. How are you feeling at the moment? How is the pain?'

He examined me, pushing his hands down in different places across my abdominal area, causing me to wince each time.

'We're going to arrange a colonoscopy for you, so we'll be putting you on a fluid only diet until this is completed. You'll be with us for a few days, I'm afraid, until we can find out what's causing this pain.'

Time passes slowly in a hospital bed. Even more so when you're in pain. The medical staff were keen to reduce my reliance on the morphine, opting for IV paracetamol instead. The discomfort would come in waves, like the changing of the tide. One moment, I would feel like my old self again, able to move around and go to the toilet unaided. Next, I would be doubled over in pain, scrambling for the commode before I would inevitably shit myself.

I could feel my nerves building as they pushed me through the long, cold corridors to the Endoscopy department. I knew the procedure would be invasive; it was unavoidable. That knowledge didn't make it any easier to mentally prepare.

I was given a sedative along with some further pain relief. All I remember after that was intense pain as the camera was inserted. I felt as though I was going to explode whenever they pumped air into my bowels in order to move the camera further along.

I remember the overwhelming sense of relief as I returned to my side room on the ward. A few hours passed and thankfully I was able to eat some food now that the investigations had been done. Doctor Ahmed arrived in the middle of the afternoon with the detailed results.

'Miss Melrose, from our investigations we have found that you have ulcerative colitis. This is a condition where the colon becomes inflamed and the lining develops ulcers.'

No cushioning.

No softening.

Just straight out with it.

At that moment, the world seemed to slow down. Doctor Ahmed continued to talk, but I couldn't process anything. I was there in body only.

'We'll start you on a course of prednisolone steroids…'

I had been healthy all my life.

'There are a few side effects that come with these…'

Now I was being told that I had an illness with no known cure. I would probably be on and off medication for the rest of my life and flare ups could happen at any time and any place. It was as if I had been running, turned a corner and been met with a wall. Everything stopped with a crash.

My head began to overload with question after question.

How can I tell people about this?

What would my family say?

Would I still be able to carry on with my police job?

Would this eventually kill me?

Once everyone had left the room, I just laid there, with my head turned to the side, staring out of the window, wishing I was someone else.

***

The clock hands in my new home were just passing half eleven by the time I was able to break free from the flashbacks and bring myself back to the present. I was still in a heap on the floor. After trialling a few small movements, I found that I was comfortable enough to try standing again. I gingerly lifted myself up, using the worktop as a support. The paracetamol was doing enough to take the edge off, but I knew that it wouldn't keep the pain at bay for long.

I slowly shuffled into the living room towards a box labelled "Kitchen" and lifted the cardboard flaps up, removing a travel mug, kettle and a rectangular tin. I headed back to the sink, moving as if I was walking on hot coals, each step causing me to cry out in pain.

With the kettle filled, I plugged it in next to the cooker and pushed down the switch. As the water heated up, I opened the tin and took out a peppermint tea bag and dropped it into the mug. When I had been in this state before, I had found the effects of a peppermint tea soothing. My next method of defence after this would be to have a bath.

I left the tea bag to soak in the boiling water, whilst I went into the front room again and opened the box containing items for the bathroom. Everyone had laughed at my colour coded labelling, but in my current condition it made a massive difference to be able to find things quickly. My mobility was increasing, but I didn't want to overdo it. I took a few items from the "Bathroom" box, including a towel, which I slung over my shoulder and went back into the kitchen and picked up my tea on the way through to the hall.

I had to tackle the stairs one at a time, stepping up with my right leg first, then bringing my left alongside it, trying not to spill my drink or drop anything. It was a relief when I reached the top; an achievement, even.

Thankfully, I had arranged for a cleaner to give the house the once over before I moved in, so the bath was sparkling. I pushed down the plug and turned on the taps, pouring in a few drops of bubble bath from one of the bottles I had brought with me.

After using the toilet, I put the lid of the seat down

and sat on top of it, sipping my peppermint tea as I watched the water level in the bath rise slowly. My stomach was still aching and tender to touch, but it felt like the tea was helping.

Over the years you come to understand your body and your condition. What works for one person might not work for another. But for me, this routine had been effective before, so I clung to it like a kid holding desperately onto a climbing frame.

I was overcome by a sense of calm as I carefully stepped over the side and lowered myself into the bath. The frothy bubbles tickled my chin as I leant my head across the back ledge and gazed up at the ceiling.

How different this picture was now, compared with thirty minutes ago. That was how quickly it could change. From nowhere, I could be living my life like any other normal person and then, bam! I would be doubled over, holding my stomach, or rushing to find the nearest toilet before the inevitable happened.

Stupidly, I had thought (or perhaps, hoped) that by moving here, I would leave all those troubles behind. A new place, a new me. But, that's not how living with a long-term illness works. Particularly one that other people are often unaware of. It becomes the invisible baggage that never leaves your side.

I swirled my hands around in the water, pushing the bubbles into different shapes. Distraction was also a useful recovery method during a flare up. Part of the battle is in the mind.

The bathroom door slowly opened and I could see Chester's tail bobbing along above the edge of the bath, like a shark's tail fin. I peered over to where he was now sat, looking up at me.

‘I’m much better now, Chester,’ I reassured him, ‘but thank you for checking on me.’

He remained for a few seconds, before yawning and trotting back out onto the landing. I took a few more sips of my tea, placing the empty cup on the floor tiles once I had finished. My energy levels had been drained from my body and my eyelids grew heavier.

I hooked my toe around the chain of the plug and pulled it towards me. There was a loud gurgling noise as the water began escaping down the pipes. Gingerly, I stood up and wrapped myself in the towel I had brought upstairs.

I made my way across to the master bedroom, only realising as I stepped inside that I hadn’t made the bed yet. Even so, this hadn’t prevented Chester from making himself comfortable, as he lay sprawled across the mattress fast asleep.

I sighed to myself and returned back downstairs. Thankfully, I was able to find a dressing gown and throw from one of the boxes and decided to use the sofa as a temporary bed for the night.

As I plugged my phone in to charge, I quickly scrolled through the menu and opened one of my apps. Working across London, I had slowly developed my own internal GPS, containing the whereabouts of all the closest toilets in the event of an emergency. Now I had been placed in unfamiliar territory, I knew that I would need help to begin with.

On the train journey down, I had taken advantage of the onboard Wi-Fi and downloaded one of the highest rated toilet finder apps. Within a few clicks, a map loaded displaying all the toilets in the area. It may sound silly, but it was reassuring to see so many toilet icons pop up. I exited the app, slightly more relaxed. After my episode this evening, that peace of mind was more important than ever.

The streetlight shone across my legs through a small gap in the living room curtains. I curled up beneath the blanket and turned my body to face the cushions along the back of the sofa. The pain had eased and another mild flare up had all but gone. I knew it wouldn't be the last. I couldn't fight the tiredness anymore and a few minutes after closing my eyes, I was asleep.

10

DCI Melrose sat upright with a startle, awoken by the sound of her doorbell. Daylight was streaming in through the window and after a quick check of her phone, she realised she had overslept.

The doorbell rang again.

'Just a minute!' shouted DCI Melrose, scrambling to her feet and tying up her dressing gown before rushing into the hallway. She quickly scraped her fingers through her hair, ruffling it vaguely into place, before opening the door.

'Good morning, DS Stanford.'

'Good morning, DCI Melrose.' He stuttered slightly as he spoke, with a hint of embarrassment in his voice. 'I'm so sorry, am I early?'

'Not at all. I just need to get dressed, then I'll be ready to go. Would you like to wait in the living room? It's a bit of a mess with all the boxes, sorry.'

'Thanks, that would be great,' he said, stepping inside and closing the front door behind him.

'Well,' said DCI Melrose awkwardly, 'the living room is in there, just make yourself at home and, er, I'll go and get dressed.'

DS Stanford folded the throw that had been abandoned on the sofa into a neat bundle before sitting down. He could hear the floorboards creaking as DCI Melrose ran around upstairs.

'Miaow!'

Chester came marching into the front room, pausing for a second to look DS Stanford up and down, before trotting over and rubbing up against his legs.

'Chester!' called DCI Melrose as she rushed down the stairs. 'Leave the poor man alone.'

DS Stanford chuckled. 'Don't worry about me, I love cats. We had a tabby when I was growing up called Buttons. She used to terrorise the neighbourhood. Rough night?'

DCI Melrose saw the folded throw on the sofa arm and felt herself going red.

'Yes, unfortunately I had forgotten to make my bed when I left for the museum in the morning and it was quite late by the time I got home last night. I decided to take the easy option and curled up there. It was surprisingly comfy. Well, it was either that or the sofa at work!'

DCI Melrose walked into the kitchen and put a bowl of food on the floor for Chester and refreshed the tub of water sat next to it. DS Stanford stood up and walked across to join her.

'I stopped by the office on the way over and picked up the address for Alice Browning, Professor Hail's ex-wife. She reverted to her maiden name after the divorce. Whilst I was there, I asked DC North to get in contact with Professor Stone and let him know that we need to talk to him.'

'Excellent, thank you. Well, let's see what we can find out from Alice then, shall we? Goodbye Chester.'

The cat followed the detectives to the front door and waited until they had left before returning back upstairs to fall asleep again.

'That's a cute cat you've got there.'

'Chester? Don't be fooled by the face. He's a pain most of the time. But he keeps me company and it wouldn't be home if he wasn't there waiting for me. Do you have any pets?'

'Does a cactus count?' laughed Jack.

'Low maintenance, won't make a noise, doesn't cost the earth – sounds like a smart choice to me,' smiled Kate, as they both got into the car.

'Alice lives on the other side of town, it'll take around 15 minutes or so to get there, depending on the traffic,' said DS Stanford, turning the keys in the ignition.

'What's the morning rush hour like here?'

'Probably not the same as in London. Most people work out of town, so a lot of the cars will be going in the other direction, but it can still get busy near the seafront.'

As they pulled away, Kate noticed that Rachel was just walking out of her house. They waved to each other as the car passed her driveway, before heading to the end of the road. The sun was doing its best to creep out from behind a wall of fluffy white clouds. Every now and then, a ray of light would manage to escape through a gap and cause Kate to squint. As she shuffled forward in her seat to flip the visor down, she could feel that her stomach was still tender. She tried to take her mind away from the discomfort by looking out of the window at the variety of sights they drove past.

The road along the seafront ran parallel with the promenade. A few early birds were already up and about – two mums were pushing prams side by side as they walked along chatting, an elderly man was sat on a bench staring out to sea and a runner was sprinting by.

The tide was out – merely a thin line in the distance, leaving the golden sand exposed. A group of people were exercising on the beach, running on the spot at first, then switching to star jumps before dropping to the ground to complete a series of gruelling press ups.

As they drove further along, the car passed the wooden pier. The multi-coloured lightbulbs surrounding the entrance were already flashing in different sequences. A few of the shops were just beginning to lift their shutters and open up. A small queue had already formed outside the coffee kiosk.

'What do we know so far about Alice Browning?' said DCI Melrose.

'She was married to Professor Hail for fifteen years, but they divorced just under a year ago.'

'I wonder why they split after fifteen years. Seems a long time to stay with someone before realising you're not meant to be together.'

'Maybe he cheated on her. Or she cheated on him. Or they simply grew apart. It does happen.'

'Speaking from experience, DS Stanford?'

'Not quite,' he laughed.

'And what was it that Georgie Westbrook overheard?' said DCI Melrose. 'That he was on the phone to Alice and said the word "stalker"?'

'We don't know for certain that he was on the phone to Alice, though. She only heard him say the words "Alice" and "stalker".'

'Why would you stalk your ex-husband?'

'Maybe she still wanted to be with him and couldn't let go?'

'Either that or Professor Hail was telling Alice about a stalker. Perhaps he was confiding in her.'

DS Stanford turned the car down a narrow side road that led to a bridge across the harbour entrance. Rows and rows of boats were lined up along the pontoons. A fishing boat was just returning with the morning catch, causing the other vessels to bob up and down as the movement disturbed the water.

When the car had reached the other side of the bridge and turned left, Kate could see an old looking stone building, grey in colour and with a curved entrance. There were patches of green dotted along the surface, where tufts of grass and plants had grown through the gaps in the brickwork.

'What's that building over there?'

'It's a fort, built during the war. They've turned it into a museum now. Worth a look around, it's quite interesting learning about the history of the town.'

'I'll have to check it out one day. How much further do we have?'

'Not long now. She lives on one of the roads at the top of this hill. So, this is officially day one of your new job. Congratulations! I bet you didn't think you'd be thrown head first straight into a murder inquiry, did you?'

'I'm used to the job interfering with life, but I had hoped to at least unpack before starting. Although, I am seeing the sights and meeting new people,' said Kate, wryly. 'It's just nice to be out of London.'

'I hope you don't mind me asking,' said Jack, 'but why did you choose to leave the city? Surely there are plenty of opportunities for a talented detective like you in the big smoke?'

'It's a long story. I just needed a change of scenery.'

DS Stanford could tell from the tone of her voice that DCI Melrose didn't want to discuss this any further. He took the hint and dropped the subject, just as he began turning left into a small cul-de-sac. Towards the end of the road, they pulled up outside a large detached house and DS Stanford switched the engine off.

'Nice house,' said DCI Melrose. 'Can't be short of money then.'

'This was the house she shared with Professor Hail. He gave it to her in the divorce.'

'He gave her a house? I didn't realise how much money there was in museum work.'

DCI Melrose and DS Stanford stepped out of the car, closing the doors behind them. The curtains of the neighbouring house twitched slightly as they walked down the driveway.

'Another audience, I see,' said DCI Melrose, as she rang the bell.

The door opened and a blonde woman in her mid-40s appeared. Her eyes looked heavy and her cheeks were red and swollen.

'Ms Browning? My name is DCI Melrose and this is DS Stanford.'

They both held out their identification long enough for Alice to check.

'We're here to ask you some questions about your ex-husband, Malcolm Hail. Would it be OK for us to come in please?'

Alice nodded, before moving to one side and allowing them to step inside. She shut the door and led them through a short corridor to a sitting room at the back of the house. The view through the patio doors, beyond the neatly turfed garden, stretched across the entire bay.

'Malcolm always loved that view,' said Alice, gazing out through the glass. 'It's the reason we bought this house. It's a pain to get to in the summer when all the holidaymakers are queuing up on the main road. But, when you finally get home and see the sun setting across the water, it makes it worthwhile. I just wish…I'm sorry…I just can't believe this has happened.'

She dropped down onto a wooden rocking chair, bringing a tissue up to her face. DCI Melrose and DS Stanford sat down on a wicker sofa opposite her. For a while, the only noise that filled the large room was a gentle sobbing from Alice.

'Ms Browning, we're sorry for your loss and I appreciate this must be a very difficult time, but we would like to ask you some questions please,' said DCI Melrose.

'Yes…I understand,' replied Alice as she dabbed the tears away from her face and composed herself. 'Anything I can do to help catch Malcolm's killer.'

'Thank you,' said DCI Melrose. 'When was the last time you spoke with your ex-husband?'

'Erm, we exchanged a few messages last week. Just me wishing him luck for the new exhibition. But the last time I actually spoke to him was on the phone, probably just over a week ago now.'

'You haven't seen him in person recently then?' said DS Stanford.

'No, not for about a month.'

'Did your relationship end…amicably?' said DCI Melrose.

'Yes. We still loved each other very much, but his work was very demanding. Sometimes he would spend weeks or even months overseas on digs. I know it's a cliché, but you could say he was married to his job. In the end, I gave up competing with it. There are only so many times you can wait alone in a restaurant for your husband to turn up. Only so many excuses you can give to your family and friends to explain why he was absent from another event.'

Throughout the journey to the house, Kate had felt the tell-tale pains again in her abdomen. Discretely in the car she had been using the app on her phone to search for a nearby toilet and at the same time trying to fabricate a plausible reason to stop – as if the need to use the loo were such a crime. She couldn't bring herself to say anything then, but now she had no choice. She couldn't ignore the urge any longer.

'Ms Browning, I apologise for asking, but could I possibly use your bathroom, please?'

'Of course, it's at the top of the stairs on the right.'

'Thank you. Excuse me.'

Feeling her cheeks turn red, the detective scurried out of the room and quickly up to the landing, before darting into the first door on her right. Her sense of embarrassment soon shifted to a feeling of relief.

Downstairs, DS Stanford continued the questioning.

'How had Professor Hail seemed these past few weeks?'

'Like I said, he was very busy with the preparations at the museum. He would often stay there until the early hours of the morning. But he did seem a bit distracted as well. His mind was preoccupied, which wasn't like him at all. He was normally so focussed on the job.'

'Did he give any indication as to what might have been distracting him?'

'He had mentioned that he thought he was being followed.'

'A stalker?'

'Yes, that's what he thought anyway. I think he'd

received a few strange emails as well. At one point he even accused me.'

Alice managed to raise a slight laugh at the thought of this, but was quickly overcome by grief and held a tissue up to her face again.

'Did Malcolm have any idea who else it could be?'

Alice shook her head.

'Is there anything else, other than the stalker, that may have been playing on his mind?'

'He was having a book published – I know that was putting an awful strain on him. The book was effectively going to ruin the career of a rival professor.'

'Professor Stone?'

'Yes, Professor Stone. As much as Malcolm didn't like him, I think he was struggling with the idea of damaging someone's career in that way. I don't know the exact details, but during a recent dig, Malcolm had found evidence that suggested Professor Stone had been falsifying his research. If proven, it's likely he would have lost his job at the university.'

DCI Melrose felt as though she had been gone for a while, although it had only been a few minutes. As she walked back down to the hallway, a photograph of Malcolm, Alice, Edith and Georgie caught her attention. They were all dressed smartly, as if they had been at an awards ceremony or fancy ball. Malcom was in a tuxedo, with shiny black shoes and Alice was wearing a navy-blue dress, paired with an expensive looking necklace. Edith wore a burgundy maxi dress and Georgie had a black cocktail dress on, with a sparkling silver bracelet wrapped around her left wrist.

Looks like a fun evening, thought Kate, before she was interrupted by the ringing of her mobile phone.

She took it out of her pocket and looked at the caller ID before answering.

'DCI Melrose here.'

'Hi, it's DC Murphy. I've just spoken with Professor Hail's solicitor. Turns out he is also the executor of the estate. He has confirmed that Alice Browning is in the will. She's been left over half a million pounds.'

DCI Melrose whistled. 'Thank you, DC Murphy, that's really helpful to know. We'll be back to the station in a bit. How's DC North getting on with the CCTV?'

'He's had a bit of trouble there. The copies of the footage onsite at the museum are blank – it looks like there was a malfunction and either the discs weren't loaded correctly, or they didn't write to the disc successfully. DC North is now contacting the external company.'

'Thanks for the update. Speak soon.' DCI Melrose ended the call and put the phone back in her pocket, before re-joining DS Stanford and Ms Browning.

'Can you confirm where you were on Saturday night at the time Professor Hail was murdered?' said DCI Melrose.

DS Stanford shuffled slightly in his seat. Alice stared at them both for a while before quietly answering.

'You think I had something to do with this?'

'It seems Professor Hail left you a substantial amount of his estate, so we just need to confirm your alibi.'

'Malcolm drafted the will when we were married and yes, he told me what was in it. Even after the divorce he promised he wouldn't change it. I told him I didn't want a penny of his money. That's not the kind of person I am. So, if you must know, I was at my parents the whole weekend. Here are their contact details if you don't believe me.' Alice scribbled down a phone number and address and handed it across to DS Stanford. 'And, not that it's any of your business, but I've already planned what to do with the money – a new wing is being built for the museum in Malcolm's memory. I've already spoken with Edith Chapman. Like I said, I didn't want his money. Now, if you don't mind, I'd like to be left alone.'

'Thank you for your time, Ms Browning,' said DCI Melrose, standing up.

'If you think of anything else that might be of use to us, please give us a call,' added DS Stanford, holding out a business card.

Alice reluctantly took the contact details, before turning away to look out over the garden.

As the detectives were leaving, DCI Melrose stopped in the doorway and turned back.

'Sorry, Ms Browning, but I have one further question. Does the name "William Carter" mean anything to you?'

'No, I've never heard of him. Now, please. I won't ask you again. Get out of my house.'

11

'What d'you reckon then?' asked DS Stanford as he put his seatbelt on.

'She was a bit defensive when I mentioned the will. Half a million pounds is a lot of money to come into.'

'She seemed genuinely upset to me.'

'Maybe. Did you find out anything else whilst I was gone?'

'She mentioned the stalker, but didn't know who it was, nor did Malcolm. She also mentioned his new book – she said it's likely to get Professor Stone sacked.'

'Hmm, I think he needs to be our next point of call then. And then there's still the mystery of William Carter. Is it possible he could have been living a secret double life?'

The detectives sat in silence for a while, thinking this over. DCI Melrose could see out of the corner of her eye that the neighbourhood curtain twitcher had returned.

'OK, drive us back then please, DS Stanford.'

The car pulled quickly away, out of the side road and back down the hill towards the centre of town. More people were out and about now, either walking or cycling along the streets. The traffic was busier on the roads as well, but despite the extra vehicles, within fifteen minutes they were pulling into the underground car park at the police station.

'Good morning, DC North and DC Murphy. Briefing around the main board in 5 minutes please,' instructed DCI Melrose as she marched into the office.

'Tea anyone?' said DS Stanford as he diverted off towards the kitchen.

'Yes please,' said DCI Melrose.

'Two sugars, please,' said DC Murphy.

'I'm good with this, thanks,' said DC North, holding up an open can of energy drink.

'I don't know how you can drink that stuff, Joe,' said DC Murphy, turning her nose up at the thought.

'You don't want any?' laughed DC North, tilting the can towards her.

'Ugh, you child,' responded DC Murphy, pushing the can away from her face. 'Honestly, it's like working with an annoying brother.'

DCI Melrose ignored the bickering and walked over to her desk to check her emails.

'Here we go,' announced DS Stanford as he placed a tray of drinks down on a table in the middle of the room.

'Thanks,' said DCI Melrose, retrieving her cup and walking in front of the board. 'OK team, let's make a start, shall we?'

The group moved their chairs until they were positioned around the investigation board.

'DS Stanford and I have been to see Alice Browning this morning, the victim's ex-wife. Whilst there, DC Murphy kindly informed me that Ms Browning is in the will, to the sum of over half a million pounds. According to Alice, she has already decided to give the inheritance to the museum in

Professor Hail's memory, which would make the money less of a motive.'

'She could be lying,' said DC North.

'That's why we need to check it out and confirm her alibi,' said DCI Melrose. 'DC North, I understand there have been some issues with the CCTV. Can you catch us up with that, please?'

The cocky detective constable took a swig from his energy drink before jumping up.

'So, when I reviewed the discs that officers retrieved from the museum yesterday, I found they were blank. I spoke with one of the other guards at the museum and apparently this has happened several times before. There was an intermittent fault in the software when the system tried to write the recorded information onto the discs. They raised it with the security company a few times and they're currently working on a permanent fix. The good news is that the security company back everything up remotely on their servers, using a direct feed, so their copies aren't affected by the same problem.'

'And what's the bad news?' said DS Stanford.

'I can't reach anyone at the security company. I even drove down there, but the premises are locked up and there was no sign of life onsite. To be honest, it looks like a one man and his cupboard type of setup!'

'OK, keep trying,' said DCI Melrose. 'The CCTV is the only thing that might prove Max isn't mixed up in all this. Until then, we have to treat him as a suspect. DC Murphy, is there anything to report from your side?'

'Yes, I've spoken with the taxi company that collected Mrs Chapman and they confirmed that a driver took her from the museum just after 10:15 p.m.

back to her house.'

'Still doesn't mean that she didn't go back later though,' said DC North.

'Can't her husband alibi her?' said DS Stanford.

'She's widowed,' said DC Murphy.

'So, no alibi for the time of the murder then,' said DCI Melrose, as she scribbled some notes on the board. 'Anything else, DC Murphy?'

'I also spoke with the Italian restaurant, Rosa's. They remember seeing Miss Westbrook with a group of her friends, but said they left the premises just before midnight.'

'In our interview she said that she went home afterwards,' said DS Stanford, flicking through his notepad. 'But, again – no concrete alibi there.'

'OK, let's look into these two a bit further then please, DC Murphy. See what you can dig up,' said DCI Melrose.

'Will do. Oh, and our digital forensic technicians are currently going through the victim's computer and I'm liaising with the phone company as well.'

'Excellent work, DC Murphy, thank you,' said DCI Melrose. 'DS Stanford, is there anything further you'd like to add?'

'Ms Browning mentioned that Professor Hail had been receiving strange emails from someone and he thought he was being followed. Hopefully tech will be able to pull the emails and trace the sender. Ms Browning also mentioned Professor Stone. She said that Hail's book would pretty much end Stone's career.'

'OK – you and I will head up to the university this afternoon and see if we can find Professor Stone. DC Murphy, look into Ms Browning's alibi please. DC North, keep trying to get hold of the security company and once you've done that, please help DC Murphy with the background information on Mrs Chapman and Miss Westbrook. See what else you can find out about Max Roberts as well. Any luck with the name "William Carter"?'

The Detective Constables shook their heads.

'OK, well there must be something that links Professor Hail and William Carter, so let's keep looking. Well done, everyone. Let's press on.'

The group moved back to their desks and began tapping away at their keyboards. DCI Melrose picked up her phone and dialled a number.

'Hello?'

'Hello Mrs Chapman, it's DCI Melrose calling.'

'How can I help you, Detective?'

'Ms Browning mentioned that she spoke with you this morning regarding her inheritance. Can you confirm if that is correct, please?'

'That's right – she is giving the money to the museum and we're going to honour Professor Hail's legacy with a new wing in his name.'

'Did you discuss anything else?'

'Not really. I asked how she was holding up and if there was anything I could do.'

'Thank you, Mrs Chapman. I do have one more question – does the name "William Carter" mean anything to you?'

'There is something familiar about the name, but...no, sorry, I can't place it right now.'

'No problem, thank you for your help, Mrs Chapman,' said DCI Melrose, replacing the handset. 'DS Stanford, let's take a drive to the university and see if we can track down Professor Stone. I still haven't heard back from DI Swift. I'll keep chasing from my end, but DC North, perhaps you could also speak with some of your old colleagues and see what you can find out, please? We still can't rule out that our murderer was an intruder.'

'Yes, DCI Melrose,' said DC North, his voice barely containing his frustration at being given the task of reaching out to his former team.

DCI Melrose grabbed the print out of the campus map from the output tray as she left the room behind DS Stanford. The two detectives were soon back in the car and driving out of the police station.

***

'There'll be nowhere left for me to explore by the time this case is solved,' joked DCI Melrose as they pulled up to a set of traffic lights outside the gates to the university.

'I'm sure we'll be able to find somewhere for you,' smiled DS Stanford.

The road to the main car park weaved through the heart of the campus. One side of the journey was lined with a row of trees and on the other side were several large playing fields. A game of rugby was taking place on one of the pitches furthest away. DS Stanford pulled the car into a vacant space, just outside a coffee shop. Several students were sat around on benches, some reading or typing on their laptops, others chatting and sipping on drinks.

'Looks like the Department of Archaeology is this way,' said DCI Melrose, pointing towards a building beyond the far side of the car park.

A set of automatic doors slid open as the detectives approached the outside of the glass structure. Ahead of them sat a man behind a shiny reception desk, talking loudly on a headset.

‘I’ll be with you in one minute,’ he said, with one hand covering the microphone.

The detectives turned around to examine the building as they waited.

‘Nice looking place,’ remarked DCI Melrose.

‘Yeah, it didn’t look like this when I was here,’ said DS Stanford. ‘The whole campus was renovated about a year after I left.’

‘I didn’t know you were a student here, what did you study?’

‘History. The original plan was to become a teacher. You know – elbow pads on a quirky tweed jacket and all that.’

‘Yeah, I could see that,’ joked DCI Melrose. ‘Some nice corduroy trousers to match as well and a leather satchel.’

‘How can I help you both?’ said the receptionist, pulling the headset down around his neck.

‘We’re looking for Professor Arthur Stone please,’ said DCI Melrose, presenting her badge.

‘You and most of the department, I’m afraid. He didn’t show up for work today. They’ve had me calling his house all morning, but there’s been no answer.’

‘Is that normal behaviour for Professor Stone, to not turn up without notice?’ asked DS Stanford.

‘Nope,’ said the receptionist, tapping into the keyboard. ‘In fact, prior to today his attendance record has been immaculate. This is his first day absent since he’s been here. I’ve had to scramble around to contact students and try to get a covering Professor. Honestly, it’s been an absolute nightmare.’

‘Yes, I’m sure,’ said DCI Melrose, in a disinterested tone. ‘Well, if you do hear from him, can you contact us on this number please? We really need to speak with him urgently.'

'Of course. It's not anything to do with the murder at the museum, is it?'

'Why do you ask that?' said DCI Melrose.

'Well, I know that Professor Stone used to work there. I overheard him on the phone on Friday saying that he was going to the opening of the new exhibition the next day. It was no secret that there was a massive rivalry between him and Professor Hail. First, he ends up dead, then Professor Stone goes missing and now the police turn up. Doesn't take a detective to…well, you know.'

DCI Melrose and DS Stanford looked at each other before turning back to the receptionist.

'If you could just call us if you do speak with him, please,' said DCI Melrose.

'How had Professor Stone seemed leading up to the weekend?' asked DS Stanford.

'Quite agitated, actually. I couldn't understand why he would go to the exhibition opening when he always blamed Professor Hail for stealing his job at the museum. And then there was Professor Hail's new book as well.'

'What do you know about the book?' asked DCI Melrose.

'The day he found out about the book, well, he was absolutely fuming. Kept telling anyone who would listen that it was all lies and it was Professor Hail's way of ruining him for good. In fact, he spent an entire lecture going on about it – we had a lot of complaints from the students. When the head of the department went to calm him down, he stormed out shouting that Hail would pay and that he would "kill the bastard". I'm quoting, you understand. I wouldn't use that language myself, of course.'

‘Thanks for your help,’ said DCI Melrose, before turning away from the desk and walking back outside with DS Stanford.

‘It fits, doesn’t it?’ said DS Stanford, as they headed along the path to the car park.

‘He certainly has motive. Professor Stone stood to lose everything with the publishing of the book. No one remembers seeing him leave either, so if he’d hidden up in the office, he would have had opportunity. Having worked at the museum he would have also known all the different ways of getting in and out of the building.’

‘And now he has disappeared.’

‘Yes, doesn’t look good for him, does it? Let’s get back to the office and work on tracking him down. If he’s not at home, he could be staying with friends or family.’

Before DS Stanford could respond, DCI Melrose’s mobile phone began to ring.

‘DCI Melrose speaking.’

‘It’s DC North here. DI Swift emailed to say he’ll be up to brief us on the burglaries in one hour.’

‘Excellent. We’re on our way.’

12

DCI Melrose stood in the break room trying to suppress another yawn as she stirred her coffee. Fatigue was beginning to take over her body, the effects of living with a long-term condition, made all the worse by the poor quality of her sleep the previous night. She began rubbing her eyes as DS Stanford walked in.

'Are you OK, Kate? I thought you were going to fall asleep in the car driving back.'

'You should take it as a compliment for the way you drive,' she joked, trying to deflect from the truth of the matter.

'Painfully slow and mind-numbingly dull?' laughed Jack.

'No, safe and steady. It was just a bit of a rough night on the sofa,' smiled Kate.

'We'll have to make sure we get you home tonight in time to make your bed then.'

'The full autopsy report came back – the primary cause of death is listed as "traumatic aortic rupture", rather than the blunt force trauma on the back of his head and neck. There is also mention of the significant and rapid loss of blood along with multiple organ failure, all of which are consistent with the Professor's impact with the dinosaur skeleton. Death would have been virtually instant.'

‘If he had stumbled across a random intruder, hitting him on the back of the head would’ve probably been enough to disable him for a few minutes to allow them to escape. It seems like a big leap from breaking and entering, to murder.’

‘Possibly – except he had already told Mrs Chapman he had information about something. Perhaps it was the thefts. If he was working late in an attempt to catch the culprits, he could have been targeted because of that. Did we hear back about the vase?’

‘Yes – none of the prints recovered matched our exclusion prints taken from the museum staff. They ran them through the IDENT1 database but no hits came back.’

‘Likely to be nosy visitors poking around. The vase was sat out in the open in an area with lots of footfall, there could be hundreds of useless prints on there. Still doesn’t rule out someone at the museum either, if they were wearing gloves.’

‘Have you seen today’s paper?’ asked DS Stanford, reaching to open a folded copy of the Spiral Bay Gazette.

‘“Murder Mystery at the Museum”,’ read DCI Melrose, taking the newspaper and scanning the article. ‘“Professor Malcolm Hail, 44, was murdered in the early hours of Sunday morning by an unknown assailant. The Head of Palaeontology was found impaled on the head of a triceratops skeleton in the main foyer by night guard, Max Roberts. There are no suspects at present and the death is being investigated by the new detective in town, DCI Kate Melrose, a former London officer with the Metropolitan Police.”’

‘No pressure,’ smiled DS Stanford.

‘At least the picture is flattering. I guess we had better solve this case then, otherwise everyone in the town will be buying me a one-way ticket back to London.’

‘Not me,’ replied DS Stanford. ‘I’ll just drive you back there.’

DCI Melrose snorted into her cup, spraying coffee onto the floor.

‘Sorry to interrupt,’ said DC North, as he appeared in the doorway. ‘DI Swift has just arrived.’

DCI Melrose quickly mopped the floor with a kitchen towel before grabbing her mug and following DC North and DS Stanford back into the main office. A broad-shouldered man with dark hair was sat at her desk, his legs crossed over and his feet resting on top of her paperwork.

‘So, this is Little Miss London then?’ he sneered, as the group approached. ‘Glad to finally meet the bitch who stole my job.’

The room fell silent and DCI Melrose could feel all eyes were on her, waiting for her response. She lifted up DI Swift’s legs, swivelling the chair so that his body faced hers and then leaned forward towards him, dropping his legs to the ground as she placed her hands either side of him on the arm supports.

‘That’s “DCI Bitch” to you, Detective Inspector.’

The onlookers tried to suppress their laughter, as an uncomfortable DI Swift shifted slightly in the seat before standing up.

‘Yeah, well, it was just a joke, obviously,’ he said. ‘No harm intended.’

‘Let’s save the jokes for when we’ve both solved our cases, shall we?’ retorted DCI Melrose, gesturing to DI Swift to make use of a vacant chair behind him.

‘OK, but before we get down to business…North!

Make yourself useful – tea,' ordered DI Swift.

'Sir,' said DC North, leaving for the kitchen without his customary sarcastic remark or witty comment.

'DI Swift, as you know, we're looking into the murder of Professor Malcolm Hail. I understand that your team have been investigating the recent burglaries at the museum, so it would be useful if you could outline the details for us, in case we're looking for the same people.'

'The burglaries are unrelated,' replied DI Swift.

'How can you be so sure?' asked DS Stanford. 'You don't even know the details of our case.'

'I don't need to. Whoever is carrying out the break-ins wouldn't get caught up in murder, they just want to make some quick money. They're slick – in and out as if they were never even there. The only reason the museum knew there had been any thefts is because they found items missing.'

'You mean there weren't any signs of forced entry?' said DCI Melrose.

Before DI Swift could answer, DC North returned and handed him a cup of tea.

'Bloody hell!' said DI Swift, spitting the contents of his mouth out across the floor. 'I didn't ask for piss water, North. Go and get some sugar.'

DC North turned and walked back to the kitchen without saying anything.

'And bring the stash of biscuits you lot try to hide from us,' shouted DI Swift. 'Where were we? Ah, signs of entry. No. No obvious signs of forced entry. No smashed windows or broken locks. We think the most likely entry point was through the loading bay out the back, that's the weakest point of the museum perimeter, but barring a few scratches and dents, you know, usual wear and tear on the shutter, there wasn't anything to confirm our suspicions.'

'Well, then it must have been an inside job, someone with a key, like one of the staff,' said DS Stanford.

'Wrong again. We interviewed them all, checked all their alibis. I do know how to run an investigation, you know?'

'Did you look into their financials for any unusual activity?' said DS Stanford.

'Did you not hear me? Alibis checked out. No point wasting time and resources combing through the bank accounts.'

'What about the items that were stolen? Have any been recovered?' asked DCI Melrose.

DC North returned with a pot of sugar and some biscuits on a plate.

'Finally!' said DI Swift. 'I thought maybe you'd decided to bake them yourself since you were taking so bloody long.'

'The stolen items, DI Swift?' reiterated DCI Melrose, trying to bring his attention back to the matter at hand.

'Nothing has been recovered yet. We trawled through the CCTV – waste of time that was though, they've probably got the most antiquated system in the country. Half the cameras don't work, the other half are grainy. We had to get most of the footage directly from the security company and they were about as useful as a...Look, if you ask me, the museum have made themselves an easy target, it's no wonder they got broken into. Crimes like this are ten a penny. There's no chance of catching them.'

'Yes, well I'm sure they'll find that comforting,' said DCI Melrose, dryly. 'Did you not find any prints?'

'Yes, we did,' said DI Swift. 'It's a fucking museum, we found hundreds of them. Look, I've emailed you a copy of our notes, do you need anything else? Because I do actually have a job and a team to get back to. And, quite frankly, I'd rather not hang about here much longer – this room absolutely reeks.'

'I've no doubt the smell will sort itself once you're gone,' said DCI Melrose. 'Thanks for your…help. I wouldn't want to keep you from your team any longer. I'm sure they're missing you.'

DI Swift slowly stood up, brushing the biscuit crumbs off of his suit and onto the floor.

'It's been a pleasure, DCI,' he said through gritted teeth. 'North – make yourself useful and wash my cup up.'

The team watched as the Detective Inspector walked out of the room, allowing the door to slam shut behind him.

'I think he likes me,' joked DCI Melrose, as DC Murphy walked in through a door at the other end.

'What did I miss?' she asked.

'Just a visit from the station's happiest Detective Inspector,' laughed DS Stanford.

'Not much then,' smiled DC Murphy, walking over and sitting at her desk.

'I'll have a read through of their notes, but it doesn't sound like they've got much, does it?' said DCI Melrose.

'I wouldn't be surprised if they bodged the investigation,' chimed in DC North. 'He doesn't care about a case if he doesn't think he can close it.'

'Did you get any useful information at all?' said DC Murphy.

'Not really,' answered DS Stanford. 'They have no suspects, there's no decent CCTV, no usable prints, none of the items have been recovered. Oh, and there weren't any signs of forced entry. Swift said they interviewed all the staff and ruled them out, but it has to be one of them. How else would someone get in and out of a museum leaving no trace? You'd have to know the place like the back of your hand.'

'It's not our case to solve,' said DCI Melrose. 'We're already looking into the staff at the museum, but make sure you check their financials too. See if we can find any evidence of unexplained sums of money being deposited. DC Murphy and DC North – can I leave that with you to arrange please?'

'Yes, DCI Melrose,' they responded, simultaneously.

'DS Stanford, can you check in with the university please? See if Professor Stone has made any further contact. If not, start calling anyone related to him. Someone must know his whereabouts.'

'On it,' said DS Stanford, moving across to his desk and unlocking his PC.

DCI Melrose sat down at her seat and scrolled through the rows of emails in her inbox until she found the one sent by DI Swift. She double clicked on the attachment and began to make notes as she read.

'OK, thank you for your help. If you do hear anything more, please call me on this number,' said DS Stanford before replacing the receiver and looking across to DCI Melrose. 'I just spoke with one of Professor Stone's neighbours.'

'And?'

'They said that he left his house on Sunday morning carrying a holdall and hasn't been back since.'

'Interesting,' said DCI Melrose. 'He's definitely doing a good job of making himself look guilty. Circulate a description; let's see if one of the patrols spot him. If we've got nothing by tomorrow, we'll do a press release with his photo and try to flush him out that way.'

'Will do,' replied DS Stanford, picking up the phone once again.

The rest of the afternoon passed by quickly; the office maintained a steady buzz of noise with the intermittent tapping of keyboards and occasional phone call increasing the volume every now and then.

Most of DCI Melrose's time was spent reading through her interview notes and adding comments to the investigation board. Her stomach had begun twinging in the early hours of the evening and she was grateful to have been office based with easy access to the toilet, avoiding the need to make excuses, or the embarrassment of having to rush away quickly.

She sat back in her chair, sipping on what seemed like her tenth coffee of the day, trying desperately to keep her eyelids from closing. The rest of the team were working hard at their desks. She found the atmosphere strangely hypnotic. As she continued to watch them, each of her blinks became longer and longer and soon she had drifted to sleep.

'OK, let's get a PCA with morphine set up and a bag of fluids,' said Doctor Ahmed, speaking to the nurse stood next to him. 'Let's get some blood samples to the lab for testing as well. Kate? Can you hear me? You're having a bad flare up; we need to get the pain under control and replace the fluid you've lost. I think the best thing is to get you transferred to the Gastro ward, OK? Nurse, we need to start a course of steroids as well, please, begin with 40mg of prednisolone. Kate? Kate?'

DCI Melrose woke up with a start to find DS Stanford stood beside her, shaking her shoulder.

'Are you OK? I was calling you from across the room and when I walked over you had a very distressed look on your face. Bad dream?'

'Something like that,' replied DCI Melrose, her cheeks red with embarrassment. 'How are you getting on?'

'I've released the description of Professor Stone. Nothing back yet. DC North and DC Murphy are just arranging everything to get access to the financial records of the museum staff. Do you want me to drive you home? You don't look too well.'

'Thanks, yes, I suppose I should go back and make a proper bed for tonight. I'll carry on with my work at home.'

DCI Melrose stood up and began packing her bag. Outside the window she could see nothing except darkness, broken only by the occasional flash of light as a car passed by. The two detectives left the investigation room and made their way downstairs to the underground car park.

'Shit, that's cold,' said DCI Melrose, as they stepped out into the open parking structure.

'Yeah, I think the next few days are going to be chilly,' said DS Stanford, unlocking the car as they approached the doors. 'And the forecast says we'll have rain for the rest of the week.'

'Perfect. I'd better chuck an umbrella in my bag for the morning then,' replied DCI Melrose. 'Tomorrow is going to be another busy day, that's for sure. I don't want to be sat in the office soaking wet!'

'Yes, the tech team should hopefully have

something for us from Professor Hail's computer. They're currently trawling through his hard drive and emails,' said DS Stanford, as he drove the car out onto the main road in front of the police station.

As they passed along the seafront, the promenade was lit up with rows of lights all twinkling in a sequence. The moonlight was shimmering off the sea; the water gently breaking onto the beach before trickling back out. A man and woman were braving the low temperature and walking briskly across the sand, followed closely by their dog, who kept straying too close to the water and then running frantically away as the waves came in.

The car came to a stop at a set of traffic lights a short distance from the museum. DCI Melrose took her mobile phone out of her pocket and began to scroll through her personal emails. A few minutes passed before the lights turned green and DS Stanford pulled slowly away. As the car was passing the museum, DCI Melrose glanced up. Through one of the windows, a flickering light caught her attention and she twisted in her seat to look back at the building as it disappeared into the distance.

'Jack, turn the car around, please.'

'What? Why?'

'We need to go back to the museum. I think I just saw something.'

DS Stanford checked his mirrors and indicated, before completing a U-turn. They were soon pulling into the car park of the museum, where DS Stanford turned off the engine and lights.

'Look! Up there,' said DCI Melrose, pointing to one of the windows along the front. They could see a light flickering intermittently, as if a torch was being shone around the room.

'I would say that's roughly where Professor Hail's office is, wouldn't you?' said DCI Melrose.

'It could just be the guard on one of their patrols. Or one of our uniformed officers, checking everything is clear?'

'That room is a crime scene, DS Stanford. No one has any business being in there, except us. Let's get inside and take a look.'

The detectives stepped out of the car and DS Stanford walked to the rear to open the boot.

'Here you go,' he said, holding out a torch and baton. 'I always keep a spare.'

'Were you a boy scout, by any chance?' laughed DCI Melrose. 'Let's go.'

When they arrived at the main door, DS Stanford tried the handle.

'Locked. I'll push the buzzer and see if we can get the guard's attention.'

After a few seconds, a voice could be heard from the speaker.

'Hello?'

'This is DS Stanford and DCI Melrose from the police. Can you let us in please?'

'Certainly, one moment please.'

A few seconds later, a key was turning in the lock and the door opened. The guard looked at their ID before letting them both into the main hall.

'How can I help you?' asked the guard.

'Have you just been upstairs?' said DCI Melrose.

'No, my next patrol isn't for another hour or so.'

'Is anyone else in the building with you?' checked DS Stanford.

'No. It's just me.'

'Where's the officer that should be here to preserve the crime scene?' asked DCI Melrose.

'An urgent call came through for a domestic disturbance in a house up the road and apparently dispatch told him there were no other officers available, so he had to respond.'

'OK, wait down here please and lock the front door again. Don't let anybody leave, OK?' said DCI Melrose, nodding to DS Stanford to follow her as she walked across to the stairs.

They passed the dinosaur skeleton, now cordoned off by tall, wooden boards, and began their ascent. As they approached the top, they both turned on their torches. Although the lights were on in the main hall, the first-floor balcony was dimly lit.

A few moments later, they had turned left into the corridor by Professor Hail's office. Carefully, they crept along, trying to suppress any noise from the floor until they were stood either side of the professor's door. DCI Melrose pointed downwards, to where light was spilling out from the room through a small gap between the floor and the foot of the door. The police tape that had originally stretched across the opening from one side to the other, had been ripped in half. DCI Melrose wrapped her knuckles on the door.

'This is the police! Please step out of the office, keeping your hands where we can see them.'

The light suddenly went off and there was silence for a few moments, before the sound of glass smashing filled the air. DCI Melrose nodded to DS Stanford, who turned the handle and barged into the room, shouting as he did so.

'Police! Stop where you are!'

A man in a balaclava was trying to force open one of the windows. His hand was bleeding from where he had punched through one of the panes.

‘Turn around slowly, keeping your hands above your head,’ ordered DCI Melrose.

The man stepped back from the window and suddenly charged in the direction of DS Stanford, bundling him across the room. DCI Melrose drew the baton from her coat pocket and swiped through the air at the assailant’s knees, bringing him crashing to the ground.

‘You OK, Jack?’

‘Yeah, I’m fine,’ said DS Stanford, lifting himself off the ground and wiping the blood away from his nose.

He walked across to DCI Melrose, who had cuffed the intruder and was hauling him onto his feet. DS Stanford grabbed the bottom of the black, woollen face covering and lifted it up until the man’s face was no longer hidden.

‘Well, well. We’ve been looking for you everywhere, Professor Stone.’

13

'Here, use this to patch up your nose,' said DCI Melrose, holding out a bottle of antiseptic liquid and some cotton wool balls. 'You took a nasty knock there. Are you sure you don't want to get checked out at the hospital?'

'No, I'm fine, thank you,' said DS Stanford, dabbing around his nostrils.

They were both sat in front of the monitors in the security office of the museum, a green first aid box lying open in front of them. The proof copy of Professor Hail's book had been placed in an evidence bag, which DCI Melrose had retrieved from the car. Behind them on the sofa, Professor Stone waited, his hands still locked together in handcuffs behind his back.

The guard entered the room carrying a tray of drinks. DCI Melrose lifted up a mug of coffee and took a sip. 'Thank you, Mr…?'

'Winter, ma'am. Mr Jeremy Winter,' the guard replied.

'Thank you, Jeremy,' said DS Stanford, reaching out for his drink.

DCI Melrose picked up her mobile phone and left the room. DS Stanford continued cleaning up his wound, until she returned a few minutes later.

'OK, there's a car on the way to collect Professor

Stone,' said DCI Melrose, as she placed her phone back inside her coat pocket.

'It's not what you think,' interrupted Professor Stone.

The detectives looked at each other, before turning their chairs to face him.

'OK, what do we think?' said DCI Melrose.

'You think I murdered Professor Hail.'

'Why would we think that?' said DS Stanford.

'Because everyone knew I hated him. His book was going to ruin me.'

'What were you doing in his office then?' said DCI Melrose.

'I came to the exhibition opening on Saturday and I sat there watching that imbecile lapping up all the praise and applause and I snapped. I wanted him to feel what it's like to have the rug pulled from under you. So, when they all went into the exhibition, I snuck up to his office and stole the proof copy of his book. When I saw the news the next day, I knew how it would look if I was found with it, so I decided to lay low for a bit, until I thought I could sneak back into the museum and return it without being caught.'

'That worked out well then,' mocked DS Stanford. 'How did you even get in here without alerting the guard?'

'I hid in one of the exhibitions near to Professor Hail's office and waited until the museum had closed. Look, I didn't murder anyone, OK? I didn't. You have to believe me.'

'That explains getting inside, but how did you get through the building without being seen on the CCTV?' said DCI Melrose.

'There are a few routes through the building that avoid the security cameras if you get your timings right. The staff used to joke about how poor the system was. Everyone knew, but the museum couldn't afford anything better.'

'I'll need you to draw those routes for us when you get back to the station,' said DCI Melrose.

'How did you plan to get out?' said DS Stanford.

'Via the loading bay. All the doors have emergency release overrides, so you don't need any keys from the inside.'

DCI Melrose leaned across to DS Stanford. 'This could potentially explain how the burglars were able to get in and out of the museum as well. They could have been disguised as visitors, hidden somewhere until the museum had closed and then escaped through the loading bay with the stolen goods. DI Swift will be pleased, if he can remember how to smile.'

DS Stanford suppressed a chuckle, before focussing back on Professor Stone. 'How did you plan to get past the police officer we had left guarding the office?'

'I was going to cause a distraction. You know – push one of the display cases over, or something. Then sneak into the office whilst they were both investigating. Thankfully, your officer was called away and the security guard had just completed a patrol, so getting the book back was easy.'

DCI Melrose decided to shift the questioning elsewhere. 'Where were you on Saturday night, between 10 p.m. and 3 a.m.?'

'I was at home.'

'Alone?'

'Yes, alone.'

'Can anyone else confirm that you were at home?'

'No, I live by myself.'

DCI Melrose shuffled in her seat. 'When was the last time you spoke to Professor Hail?'

'He called me just after 10 p.m. on Saturday, swearing his head off about the book. He knew I'd taken it. He sounded like he'd had a few by then, slurring his words. He always was a miserable, violent drunk. I knew that I couldn't stop the book being published, but hearing the anger in his voice, it was enough to know that I'd rattled him, maybe even stalled him for a while.'

'Well, he's permanently stalled now and that's worked out pretty well for you, hasn't it?' said DS Stanford.

'I didn't kill him!'

'You have no alibi, Professor Stone. We know there was bad blood between you two. You stole a copy of his book from his office and then you broke into a crime scene this evening and assaulted a police detective. You can understand why this doesn't look good for you, right?' said DCI Melrose.

'Yes, but…you have to believe me. I didn't kill him. Whether or not Professor Hail is alive, that book will still be published. I will still be ruined. What would be the use in killing him? Besides, I'm not the only person who was in his office on Saturday night.'

'Who else was there?' asked DS Stanford.

'I don't know who it was. But, when I went up to his room to steal the book, I could hear someone inside, searching the office. They were looking for a good few minutes before they gave up and left. I was hiding around the corner, but I managed to catch a glimpse of them from behind as they walked away. I couldn't see much because it was quite dark in the corridor, but I could tell it was a woman. Once they had gone out of sight, I went into the office, grabbed the book and then got out of there.'

'And you didn't recognise the person at all?' checked DS Stanford.

'No, sorry. Like I said, I couldn't really see in the darkness. Whatever they were looking for they either found or gave up trying to find, but the office didn't look like it had been disturbed. Everything had been put back neat and tidy.'

'This still doesn't help with an alibi for the time of the murder, Professor Stone,' said DCI Melrose. 'We know you were at home at the time of the phone call with Professor Hail – that we can prove. But how do we know the call didn't provoke you into coming down to the museum to confront him face to face? You would have had plenty of time to get here.'

'I'm not a murderer, Detective Melrose. Yes, I was angry and I was scared that I was going to lose everything, but I wouldn't kill anyone.'

A buzzing noise interrupted the conversation.

Jeremy walked over to the main console and pushed a button. 'Hello? Can I help you?'

'It's the police. We're here to collect Professor Stone.'

'I'll be right out,' said Jeremy, before pushing the button again and leaving the security office.

'That's your ride to the station, Professor,' said DCI Melrose. 'Is there anything else that you want to tell us?'

'I have a theory about who the person in the office may have been.'

'Go on,' said DS Stanford.

'Well, I'm not sure if you've looked into Edith Chapman yet, but she's also got an axe to grind with Professor Hail.'

'In what way?' asked DCI Melrose.

'I heard on the grapevine that he was going to be taking her job as director of the museum and I think that it was her in his office that night looking for evidence so she could confront him.'

'OK, thank you, Professor Stone. The officers will take you down to the station and detain you overnight, do you understand?' said DCI Melrose.

The professor nodded his head in acknowledgement as two uniformed police constables entered the office and took him away.

'First thing tomorrow, get in touch with his neighbour again. See if they remember when he came home on Saturday night and if they heard him leave again before Sunday morning. And let DI Swift know what we've found out this evening as well, please.'

DS Stanford took a notebook from his pocket and jotted the requests down.

'Thank you for your help, Mr Winter.' DCI Melrose extended her hand towards the guard.

'My pleasure, ma'am.'

The detectives left the security office and made their way back to the car.

'What do you reckon then? Professor Stone guilty?' asked DS Stanford, as he dropped down onto the driver's seat.

'Like he said, he had nothing to achieve from killing Professor Hail. And, if he had killed him, why would he then go back to the scene of the murder to return a stolen book?'

'If his neighbour provides him with an alibi then I guess we're back to square one.'

'That's the way job goes sometimes, unfortunately. You think you're getting somewhere and then it can all fall apart and you're left with nothing. But don't forget, we haven't ruled out Max or the other museum employees yet. We still have plenty of irons in the fire. North and Murphy are already widening their nets with the background checks, so we might get lucky with one of those. I'll speak with Edith Chapman tomorrow and ask if it was her that had been inside Professor Hail's office and whether she knew about him replacing her.'

Once they pulled out of the museum car park, most of the journey back to DCI Melrose's house was spent in silence. Both detectives were starting to feel the effects of a long day. The adrenaline that had previously been coursing through DCI Melrose's veins had by now subsided and the fatigue from her ulcerative colitis had returned with a vengeance. DS Stanford could still feel his face throbbing from the impact with Professor Stone. Both just wanted to get home and rest.

'Well, here you are.' DS Stanford indicated as he pulled the car alongside the opening to DCI Melrose's driveway.

'Thank you for chauffeuring me around today. I just felt it would be much quicker than you directing me.'

'No problem. Same time again tomorrow?'

'Actually, I was thinking about walking in.'

'What about the rain?'

'It's only a thirty-minute walk, I reckon. I'm sure if I wrap up and have a brolly handy, I'll be OK. I might scrounge a lift tomorrow evening though, if that's OK?'

'I'll put it on the tab,' smiled DS Stanford. 'Have a good evening, Kate. Don't forget to make your bed!'

DCI Melrose laughed as she waved goodbye to her colleague and watched him drive away. Walking up towards the front door, she noticed a familiar face staring at her through the living room window.

'OK, Chester,' she said. 'Dinner won't be long.'

14

I barely had time to close the front door before I was pretty much rugby tackled by Chester, who came scurrying around the corner from the living room, galloping towards me like a fluffy pillow with legs. Not that I'm ungrateful to have the company. I've lived away from my parent's home, mostly alone, for around fifteen years now. So, being greeted with enthusiasm, even if it is by a furry cat who is only bothering with this amount of fuss in order to be fed, still makes me feel lucky.

'Come here, you giant ball of candy floss,' I said as I scooped him up off of the floor and into my cradled arms. He stared at me, his head tilted slightly to the left, as if to say, "Yes, it's great to see you, but where's my food?"

I released Chester back onto the floor and he quickly trotted into the kitchen, stopping to glance back in my direction every couple of steps, worried that I might have forgotten the evening meal routine we've perfected over the years. We may be in a new house, but the rules remained the same. I quickly grabbed the letters resting on the mat, hung my coat up in the hallway and then followed him.

'Right, which pouch would you like tonight then, mister?'

At the sound of the box opening, Chester launched

himself up against the kitchen cabinets, using his back legs to propel the front half of his body further up the cupboard door in order to carry out a closer inspection of the packet. With the contents emptied into his bowl, he weaved in and out of my legs as I walked across to place the dish down next to his water.

'Well, that's you sorted. I suppose I should eat something as well.'

I scrambled around, searching the boxes until I had successfully located and retrieved the microwave. I also stumbled across a tin of soup – one that had managed to survive the journey from London. With dinner heating up, I ran upstairs and half-heartedly made the bed. There was no way I could face another night sleeping on the sofa.

As I was walking back down to the kitchen, a series of high-pitched beeps notified me that my soup was ready to be served. I grabbed the dish from the microwave and retreated to the front room. Chester was still pre-occupied with his own dinner and he had managed to push his bowl across the tiles into the middle of the kitchen floor as he attempted to consume every single ounce.

I felt a sense of relief rush through my body as I slumped down onto the sofa, the weight of the day finally off of my feet. As I pressed back against the cushions, I closed my eyes and rotated my head slowly in a circular motion, counting in my mind as I breathed in and out.

I wouldn't say that I'm a strong believer in the power of meditation, but I've always found the breathing exercises useful during flare ups and in combating stress in general. However, that's the extent of my exploration into the field. When everything around you is falling apart, or when your insides feel like they are being ripped to shreds, you hold onto anything, however big or small, that gives you a sense of control. For me, it's the breathing.

I brought the bowl of soup closer to my mouth and blew across the surface, watching the steam flitter up into the air. I grabbed my notebook from my bag and started flicking through my scribbles as I began to slurp my way through my meal.

I decided to draw out a rough timeline of the case up until now, marking all the comings and goings of the people we'd spoken to so far. This highlighted a concerning gap around the time of the murder, where alibis for many of them were thin or non-existent. I continued writing for a while, until my watch bleeped. I looked down to check the time – midnight.

Chester was already curled up in a ball at the other end of the sofa. I gently lifted myself off the cushions and returned my bowl to the kitchen before climbing the stairs to bed. Despite the coldness of the sheets pressing against my body, I fell asleep almost as soon as my head met the pillow.

***

'What's happening with Miss Melrose in Bay 5?'

'Just waiting for the porters to take her up to the gastro ward.'

I tried to fight against the blurriness of my eyesight and just about managed to focus on a doctor and nurse who were stood beyond the half open blue curtain that surrounded me. I tried to pull myself further up the trolley bed, but as soon as I moved, I felt a throbbing pain in my head and the room began spinning around me.

I pulled at the various wires constricting my arm movements; most of them were hooked up to me. Eventually, I found the orange call button, which I pushed as hard as my strength would allow. A bleeping noise filled the air and I saw the nurse turn to look at me. She disappeared briefly, before rushing in with a cardboard bowl, successfully reaching me just in time as I felt the nausea take over my body. Within seconds I began throwing up.

'That'll be the morphine, Kate,' said the nurse, pushing the loose hair back behind my ears.

I've been looked after by her before and, in a weird way, we've bonded over my many visits to A&E throughout the years.

'Sorry, I'm so sorry.'

'You don't need to apologise. We'll have you up on the ward shortly and we've also managed to get you your own side room.'

'Thank you. You always look after me.'

She patted me on the side of my arm, looking at me with a smile, before taking the bowl away. A few minutes passed until the porters turned up. Although to me, those seconds felt like hours.

'Miss Melrose, we're here to take you up to the ward. Do you have any personal belongings with you that we need to take with us?'

I pointed at some items on the chair next to me and one of the men gathered them together and placed them gently at the foot of the bed. The journey seemed to take forever, winding along never-ending, cold corridors and finally finishing with a lift ride to the floor above and the entrance to the ward.

Throughout the move I held a bunch of wet paper towels over my eyes to help with the dizziness and light sensitivity. The porters pushed me carefully into the side room and lowered the safety railing next to me.

'Will you be able to move yourself across to the bed, Kate?' one of them checked.

I slowly lifted myself up and slid my legs to the right until they were dangling over the side. I took a deep breath and managed to shuffle myself across to my new (and hopefully, temporary) bed.

'Thank you,' I said, almost in a whisper, as I pulled the bedsheet over me.

'Hope you feel better soon, Miss Melrose.' With that, they both left and I was alone again.

I was lucky to have a side room with my own toilet, particularly on a gastro ward. For a while I stared out of the window, drifting in and out of consciousness. Due to the pain, I found myself topping up on morphine at every opportunity and this had caused the drowsiness. As I tilted my body slightly to lie on my side, I was quickly overcome with a pain in my abdomen; one I knew all too well.

I moved as fast as I could, wrapping the fingers of my left hand around the drip stand, which doubled up as a walking aid as I shuffled across to the toilet. The need became greater with every step and as I reached out for the door handle, I felt my legs crumble beneath me and I collapsed onto the floor, about to be overcome by the urgency.

***

I let out a scream as I bolted upright in my bed at home, frantically looking around the unfamiliar room trying to work out where I was. My breathing was limited to short, rushed bursts and my eyes took a while to adjust to the dark surroundings.

I ran my hands along my arms searching for the various lines I had been hooked up to and soon realised I had been dreaming again. However, the need for the toilet still remained and I rushed across to the bathroom just in time.

When I returned, I sat on the edge of the bed and looked at my phone – 03:15. Chester wasn't anywhere to be seen, so I assumed he had remained on the sofa downstairs.

The rest of the night was spent tossing and turning, with little sleep taking place. I watched as the sun gradually reappeared in the sky and I followed its path, climbing higher every hour, until it was time for me to get dressed for work.

'No sign of the rain that was forecast then,' I said to Chester as I put his breakfast down in front of him.

I quickly devoured a snack bar that had been abandoned in my bag for a while, before throwing on my coat and leaving the house. A good morning for a walk, I thought to myself.

The air was fresh and crisp and the scent of the salt water drifted along from the seafront. Seagulls were standing guard across most of the rooftops, screeching at one another and watching me suspiciously as I walked down to the end of my road.

By the time I reached the promenade, the temperature had dropped and a cool breeze was sweeping in across the water. I picked up the pace in an attempt to keep myself warm. A few of the passers-by nodded or smiled at me as our paths crossed.

'DCI Melrose.'

A voice from behind stopped me in my tracks and I turned to find Edith jogging up to meet me.

'Good morning,' I said.

‘Do you mind if I walk with you?’

‘Please do. I’m on my way to the station so will be passing by the museum. How are you all doing?’

‘We’re still really shaken. I gave those closest to Professor Hail the day off yesterday, to take a little time away from the museum. Today, we’re holding a full staff meeting, just to check in with everyone.’

‘That sounds like a good idea. I’m not sure if you were alerted last night, but we picked up Professor Stone breaking into Professor Hail’s office.’

‘Professor Stone? What on earth was he doing there?’

‘Returning a stolen proof copy of Professor Hail’s book. He told us about the flaws in the security systems, how there are ways of getting about without being seen by the cameras. Is that correct?’

‘I’m ashamed to say it is. I inherited the system from my predecessor. He was notorious for cutting corners. Unfortunately, when the board see that money has been saved, they don’t really care about the method that has been taken. Not a very good justification, I know.’

‘Who else is aware of the weaknesses of the camera system?’

‘Anyone who has ever worked there since the CCTV was installed, I guess.’

‘And have you given a list of all those employees to DI Swift, for the investigation into the burglaries?’

‘Yes, but to be honest…never mind.’

‘Go on, Mrs Chapman, please.’

‘Well, I don’t want to speak ill of your colleague, DCI Melrose, but I’m not really sure he was that interested in investigating anything. He visited the museum once and looked around for all of twenty minutes and hasn’t been back since. We’ve had the odd phone call or email, but it seems like he has already written off our chances of catching the thieves.'

'I'm sorry to hear that. I'm sure you'll understand that it's difficult for me to comment any further.'

Edith nodded. As we passed by one of the beach kiosks the smell of coffee swirled around my nostrils, but I did my best to resist the temptation.

'There is one other thing I need to ask, Mrs Chapman, something that Professor Stone mentioned. Were you aware that Professor Hail was being lined up to take over your job as Director?'

'Aware?' she laughed. 'It was me who suggested Malcolm in the first place. I'm retiring, detective. He is a good fit for the role and he is, well, was, very popular with the people of this town.'

'I see. And you didn't go to Professor Hail's office on the evening of the exhibition?'

'No, I spent most of my time either in the exhibition or in my own office.'

As Edith finished this sentence, we found ourselves arriving outside the entrance to the museum.

'Thank you for the company,' she said, turning to walk into the car park.

'Likewise. I'll be in touch.'

I continued my journey to the station, hoping that today would be a day of answers.

15

'Good morning, boss,' said DC North, as DCI Melrose entered the investigation room. DS Stanford quickly stood and walked over to meet the senior detective at her desk.

'Good morning, Kate. Did you manage to sleep a bit better last night?'

'Yes, thank you. First time in the new bed and managed to get a few more hours than on the sofa. How are you this morning?'

'I'm good, thank you for asking. I've briefed DI Swift on our findings and I actually stopped by Professor Stone's neighbours on my way in this morning.'

'Did you learn anything useful?'

'They remember him getting home on Saturday evening. They're not completely sure of the time, but think it was approximately half eight because, and I quote, "Strictly Come Dancing had just finished". After that, they said they could hear his TV and also heard him on the phone a few times, until everything went quiet around midnight. The next time they saw him was when he was leaving his house on Sunday morning with the holdall.'

'It's not airtight, but it's probably enough. For now.'

'What do you want us to do with Professor Stone?'

checked DS Stanford.

'Charge him with B&E and also assaulting an officer, then let him go. That's all we can do with him at the moment,' said DCI Melrose. 'On my walk in this morning, I bumped into Edith Chapman. She already knew about Professor Hail taking over from her – she actually made the suggestion to the board herself.'

'Any idea who the mystery woman was visiting his office?' said DS Stanford.

'According to Edith, it wasn't her. Judging from the list of attendees at the exhibition, there's a lot of other potential suspects. Over half of them were female.'

DS Stanford leaned back, his face looking to the ceiling as he rubbed his eyes. 'I can see this case being a frustrating one. Every time it feels as though we're getting close, we come up against a dead end. Considering everyone we have spoken to, barring Professor Stone, either loved or had a great deal of respect for Professor Hail, I'm beginning to wonder if there is something that we're completely missing.'

DCI Melrose could sense the disappointment in DS Stanford's tone. 'Come with me, Jack. Let's grab a drink in the kitchen.'

They both walked across the office and into the break room. DS Stanford sat down on the sofa, as DCI Melrose filled the kettle with water.

'Every case is different and it is easy to become despondent or angry when you feel as though you aren't getting anywhere,' said DCI Melrose, trying to comfort her colleague. 'Trust me, I've been there more times than I care to remember. We're doing all the right things and we're looking into all the right leads. We only have a small team and that obviously limits the number of avenues we can cover at any one time. But, when we have that "eureka" moment and everything suddenly falls into place, it will all be down to the hard work that is being done each day by people like you.'

DS Stanford smiled as he took the cup of coffee that DCI Melrose was holding in his direction.

'I'm sorry. I know I'm being impatient.'

'Don't apologise for that – it simply means you care enough about finding the culprit and bringing them to justice. Some investigations are sprints, others are marathons. And you won't always know which type of case you're on until you cross that finish line.'

'Thank you, Kate,' said DS Stanford, holding up his mug and tapping it against his colleague's. 'I guess I keep forgetting that I'm still quite junior as a Detective Sergeant.'

'Well, from where I'm standing, one could be forgiven for thinking you'd been doing this all your life. You're a natural, Jack. Just cut yourself some slack and remember to believe in your abilities. This is our first case together, but I feel like we've already started to find our groove. That can take years with some partners.'

At that moment, DC North entered the break room, sipping from a can of energy drink.

'Sorry to break up the party, but the tech team have just called. They need you to go down there.'

'Thank you. And where is "there", DC North?' asked DCI Melrose.

DC North took another sip from his drink and pointed at the floor, before heading back into the main office.

'He means the basement,' said DS Stanford,

standing up from the sofa and smoothing out his crumpled trouser legs.

'That's a bit cliché, isn't it? The tech team confined to a basement.'

'Don't feel too sorry for them, they have a better setup than anyone else in the building! Honestly, it's like something out of MI6 down there with all the gadgetry they have. Digital forensics and cyber – that's where most of the money is going these days. Crime isn't just on the streets anymore.'

DCI Melrose followed DS Stanford from the break room, cutting across the office and then through a doorway beyond their desks. In the corridor, a few officers were talking to one another. The detectives nodded as they passed by them and began descending a staircase.

They dodged several bright yellow warning signs, alerting them to the slippery floor, until they ended up outside an entrance protected by a metal grid. DS Stanford swiped his ID card and punched a number into the keypad on the wall. Following several elongated beeping noises, the door popped open slightly.

'After you,' said DS Stanford, holding the door back for DCI Melrose.

Stepping inside, Kate marvelled at the amount of equipment. The room was full of computer screens and towers. There were racks and racks of wires and accessories running along the entire length of one of the walls and another door at the far end led through to several other back rooms. In front of one of the monitors was a woman in her mid-twenties, with black curly hair tucked beneath a beanie.

'Hey, Cookie, how are you?' said DS Stanford, walking across and sitting down on a swivel chair next to her.

'Jackie!' she said spinning around and leaping across to give him a hug.

DCI Melrose remained near the doorway, initially looking on with an expression of confusion, before she gave a slight cough to draw attention to her presence.

'Oh, I'm sorry, ma'am, I didn't see you there. Hi, I'm Cookie, the Head of Digital Forensics. There are only two of us in the department, but we're your go to team for anything techie related. For some people, that also includes forgotten passwords. Naming no names…Jackie.'

The senior detective laughed as she crossed the room and met the outstretched hand of the technician.

'DCI Melrose.'

'Pleasure to meet you. You're here for the Hail case, right?'

'Yes, please. I understand you have something to show us?' said DCI Melrose, perching on one of the empty workstations behind her.

'I sure do. Before I start, on a scale of 1 to 10, how geeky do you want the details? Just so I know how to pitch.'

DCI Melrose looked at DS Stanford, before looking back at Cookie.

'Let's assume we know nothing about computers, for now.'

'Understood. Let me just alter the programme settings in my brain.'

Cookie placed her finger against her temple and made some noises, as if she was a robot processing information, before bursting into laughter.

DCI Melrose looked at DS Stanford, before returning her gaze to Cookie and allowing a slight smile to cross her lips.

'I think we're ready to download now,' said DS Stanford, laughing.

'Jackie, that's a terrible joke,' said Cookie, before turning to her PC and typing a command. 'OK…here's what we've found so far. The hard drive mostly contained museum documents, some music files, etc. nothing too interesting. However, from his recently accessed list we can see that he had been into a folder called "Evidence", saved on an external device.'

'And what was in that file?' asked DCI Melrose.

'Well, that's the problem, Melly.'

'Melly?' said DCI Melrose, barely hiding the shock in her voice.

'Rosie?' suggested Cookie, before looking up and seeing the look on Kate's face. 'Too soon for nicknames?'

'Probably best to stick to DCI Melrose for now,' advised DS Stanford. 'Basically, if the file is saved on an external device, such as a USB stick or external hard drive, we wouldn't be able to access the contents without having the physical object on which it is located.'

'Calm down, Jackie, you'll be doing me out of a job,' joked Cookie. 'But yes, in theory the Detective Sergeant is correct. Normally, we could trace the files, even without the external device. Most people don't realise that that when a file is opened, it leaves a trace on the machine.'

'But not in this case?' said DCI Melrose.

'Whatever was on the external drive must have been important because he went to great lengths covering his tracks,' said Cookie. 'Part of the hard drive has been cleaned. Not just with a free piece of software downloaded from the internet. I mean properly cleaned with professional kit. We'll keep digging though and see if we get lucky.'

'If the folder is named "Evidence", it could be related to the break-ins, perhaps?' said DS Stanford.

'He did tell Edith Chapman that he had discovered something,' agreed DCI Melrose. 'Anything else, Cookie?'

'Yes, his emails. Outside of the normal day to day communications, we found several which stood out due to the nature of their content. They get quite aggressive.'

'The stalker?' asked DCI Melrose.

'I would say so, yes. I've just forwarded a batch of them to you both so you can look over them in more detail, but they hit most points on the creepy spectrum, ranging from "You belong to me" to "Keep looking over your shoulder". In total there are about 30 of them, sent over the past few months.'

'Do we know who sent them?' said DS Stanford.

'We've traced the IP address and I've liaised with the ISP – that's the internet service provider – and the messages all came from the same PC. They've provided the location, but that doesn't necessarily tell us who sent them.'

'Why not? If you know which PC they came from, surely that points us to the culprit?' said DCI Melrose.

'Yes, and no. The location of the PC was traced back to Spiral Bay Primary School. Since that's an open building, we have to assume the PC could have been used by several people. Without going down there and finding the actual machine, we can only be certain about the location for now.'

'Who would be emailing the Professor from a

school? Particularly threatening emails,' said DCI Melrose, turning to DS Stanford.

'Let's try to narrow it down,' he responded, picking up a phone from the desk in front of him and dialling an extension. 'DC Murphy, it's DS Stanford, calling from the basement. Yes, she's here. What? OK, wait a second. Cookie, she said thank you for the film recommendation, she's watched the whole…actually, DC Murphy, we don't really have time for this right now. No. Never mind that now. I need you to go through the list of attendees at the exhibition and see if any of them are linked with Spiral Bay Primary School. That's right. Thank you. We'll be back up shortly.'

'Good thinking, DS Stanford. Perhaps the stalker kept close to the Professor. Hidden in plain sight, as it were. Was there anything else, Cookie?'

'That's it for now, DCI Melrose.'

'Thanks for your help. Come on, Jackie, let's head back upstairs,' teased Kate, walking back towards the entrance.

DS Stanford stood up and ruffled Cookie's beanie hat playfully, before following DCI Melrose.

'Jackie! Game night soon, yeah?' asked Cookie.

'You bet! I'm on a winning streak!' said DS Stanford, smiling as he closed the door behind him.

'She seems interesting,' observed DCI Melrose, as they began walking back upstairs.

'Cookie is lovely. Don't be fooled by her quirkiness, she's incredibly skilled at her job. And the nicknames are just a term of endearment for her. If you get a nice nickname, you've been accepted.'

'Is that so, Jackie?' joked DCI Melrose.

'You should hear what she calls DI Swift!' laughed DS Stanford as they crossed the corridor and stepped back into the investigation office.

'Any luck, DC Murphy?' said DCI Melrose, as she walked over to the board and scribbled a note about the emails.

'There was a teacher from the school on the guest list – Miss Laura Da Silva. I spoke with the museum just now and they informed me that she arranged regular trips for the children and Professor Hail would often give talks to them.'

'Good work, thank you. DS Stanford, we need to get to the school to speak with Miss Da Silva. Do you know how to check the IP address of a PC?'

'I don't, but I know someone who does,' said DS Stanford, taking his phone out of his pocket and sending a text message. 'Cookie should have responded with the necessary instructions by the time we get to the school.'

'Where is DC North?' asked DCI Melrose.

'He has gone back to the security company, to see if he can speak to someone about the CCTV,' replied DC Murphy. 'Do you want me to pass a message on?'

'No, that's OK, thank you,' said DCI Melrose. 'We'll all catch up later and see where everyone has got to in the investigation. Let's go, DS Stanford.'

As the detectives turned to leave, the reception officer entered from the other end of the room and called out to them.

'Excuse me, DCI Melrose. There are a few journalists gathered in reception wanting an update on the Hail case.'

'Where are the communications team?' said DCI Melrose, turning back to face him.

'Not onsite at the moment. Sorry, ma'am.'

'That's fine, we'll take care of it. We can leave via the front entrance and give them a statement on the way.'

The detectives followed the officer out of the investigation room and into the main reception area of the station. A group of journalists and photographers were gathered together, talking to one another.

When they saw DCI Melrose and DS Stanford walking over to them, they broke out of their huddle. The photographers brought their cameras up against their faces, ready to pounce on any photo opportunities. Some of the journalists removed handheld recorders from their pockets and pushed them towards the detectives; others turned to a new page in their notepads and stood, pencils in hand, eager to make notes.

'My name is DCI Melrose and I am the Senior Officer overseeing the investigation into the murder of Professor Malcolm Hail. We have been pursuing a number of leads, but so far have not made any arrests. If any members of the public were passing by the museum either late on Saturday night or early on Sunday morning and saw anything suspicious, please contact the station. This includes anyone driving past who may have useful dash cam footage. We believe this to be an isolated incident and would like to reassure the public that there are no indications that there is any threat to the wider community. Thank you.'

DCI Melrose and DS Stanford exited via the front door and swiped through a side gate to access the car park.

'I'm guessing you've done that a few times before,' said DS Stanford.

'Yeah, I gave quite a few press statements in London. You get used to them after the first ten or so. In most cases they help our message reach a wider audience. Worst case, we'll start getting phone calls from every amateur sleuth and passer-by now and sadly most won't give us anything useful. But you never know. Perhaps someone did see a car leaving at the time of the murder, or saw someone outside behaving strangely. We might get some luck come our way.'

The detectives sat down in the car and secured their seat belts. DS Stanford was about to turn the keys in the ignition when his mobile phone buzzed in his pocket.

'It's Cookie,' he said, looking at the screen. 'She's sent through a step-by-step guide for checking the IP address on a computer. Seems fairly straight forward.'

DS Stanford returned the phone to his pocket and started the car.

'Excellent. So, game night? What sort of games do you play?'

'A mixture. Mostly geeky board games.'

'Just the two of you?'

'No, normally a small group of us – some from the station, a few of Cookie's friends. You should join us at the next one.'

'I don't know if that's a good idea. I can be quite competitive. I'm not sure if I'm ready to show everyone that side of me yet.'

'Ha, you'd fit right in with the group. But, no pressure. Consider this an open invite, whenever you want to come along.'

'Thanks, I'll keep that in mind. I'll definitely take you on in a game of chess one day. Do you know much about this school?'

'It's one of the bigger primaries in the area, around 300 children, I think. My nephew goes there and I've collected him after school a few times. He really enjoys it and they seem to have a good reputation, so I'm surprised that one of the staff is mixed up in this. Do you really think that the stalker could be our killer?'

'Depends. The contents of the emails suggest the stalker was possessive, most likely in love with Professor Hail. But leading up to his death, the wording is more sinister – perhaps the stalker became frustrated, or were worried that they were losing their perceived control over Hail.'

'So, it could be a case of "if I can't have you, no one else can". It might be a complete coincidence that Miss Da Silva teaches at the same school the emails were sent from and was also invited to the exhibition.'

'I guess there's only one way to find out.'

16

DCI Melrose and DS Stanford walked between the two entrance pillars and pushed open the door leading through to the school reception. On one side of the room, there were rows and rows of staff photographs, each one labelled underneath with their name and a short biography. DCI Melrose gestured to her colleague with a tilt of her head and they both headed over to review the pictures.

DS Stanford raised his hand and pointed towards one of the faces. 'Here's our lady, Laura Da Silva. She is in charge of the "Silver Birch" class, key stage 2. Likes: politeness, good manners and museums.'

'Dislikes: lateness, rudeness and bad behaviour,' said DCI Melrose, completing the list. 'I wonder what her views are on murder.'

'May I help you?' said a voice from behind them.

The detectives turned around to find a small lady in her sixties peering at them over the top of her red framed glasses. From the lanyard hanging down around her neck, they could see that her name was Mrs Wool, the Headteacher.

'Good morning. My name is DCI Melrose and this is DS Stanford. We need to speak with one of your teachers, Miss Laura Da Silva.'

'Is everything OK? Has something happened?'

'We would prefer to discuss that with Miss Da

Silva, please,' said DCI Melrose.

'I'm afraid she'll have begun a class; the bell's only just rung.'

'Mrs Wool, it's important that we see her now. Can you take us to her classroom please?' said DCI Melrose.

'Well, if you insist. Yes, of course. Sign the register just in front of you there please and put one of these visitor badges on. There we go. Right, if you're both ready? Please follow me.'

The trio walked through an open set of doors and turned a corner to enter another set of doors until they were at the beginning of a long corridor.

'I do hope you don't think I was being abrupt with you, DCI Melrose,' said Mrs Wool as they began passing the windows of classrooms on their way towards the Silver Birch room. 'I have a duty to my staff and, of course, my pupils as well. It could be intimidating for the children to see two detectives turn up unannounced.'

'Of course, Mrs Wool. We can be as discreet as you need. What would work best?'

'Her Teaching Assistant will be able to look after the class. I'll go in alone at first and send the children out the side door into the wild garden for a period of reflection. That way they won't be alarmed. I'll come and get you once they're gone.'

'Thank you, Mrs Wool. We appreciate your help in this matter. Before you go in, can you let me know if the teachers all have computers in their classrooms, please?'

'They do.'

'And do the teachers rotate rooms, or do they always use the same one?' said DS Stanford.

'Each teacher has their own room. The children

move around for different lessons. Why are you asking about the computers?'

'Just getting an understanding of the movement involved in a normal school day. Thank you, that's really helpful. We'll wait here until you're ready to call us,' said DCI Melrose, dispatching Mrs Wool into the Silver Birch classroom. 'DS Stanford, I'm going to make use of the facilities over there, don't go in the classroom without me.'

DS Stanford nodded and watched Kate hurry along the corridor until she had disappeared through a doorway leading to the toilets. He turned his attention to the window behind him, which overlooked the rows of desks inside the classroom. Mrs Wool was at the front, speaking to two women, one of whom DS Stanford recognised as Miss Laura da Silva; the other he assumed to be the teaching assistant. The children were at the back of the room, taking their coats off a set of pegs before lining up in single file by an exit on the far side. The conversation between the three women drew to a close and the teaching assistant walked over to the front of the queuing pupils and marched them outside. DCI Melrose returned just as Mrs Wool was coming back out of the classroom.

She paused in front of them, raising her left eyebrow. 'All yours, detectives. Perhaps you wouldn't mind stopping by my office on the way out please? Just so I can sign you out.'

DCI Melrose nodded. 'Of course. Thank you for your help.'

Mrs Wool shuffled back down the corridor, muttering to herself, as the detectives stepped inside the classroom and shut the door behind them.

'Good morning, Miss Da Silva. I'm DCI Melrose, this is my colleague DS Stanford. We'd like to ask you a few questions about Professor Hail and the museum.'

'Of course. I heard the news. It's absolutely devastating. I haven't told the children yet; I'm trying to find the best time. We were all very fond of Professor Hail, you see. I have taken the class there on school trips a few times now. He was always so good with them. Please, sit down.'

The three of them gathered around a desk at the front, just to the side of a projector screen.

DCI Melrose began. 'Miss Da Silva...'

'Please. Call me Laura.'

'OK. Laura. How well did you know Professor Hail?'

The teacher shifted in her seat slightly before answering. 'Well, of course I knew him from the visits to the museum. And, I would usually go alone first before taking the children to any exhibitions. I'd often bump into Malcolm around the galleries.'

'Did you see him outside of the museum at all?'

'Why are you asking? What does this have to do with his death?'

'We're just trying to build a picture of everyone he interacted with,' replied DCI Melrose.

'I did have dinner with him, once or twice.'

DS Stanford looked up from his notepad. 'Can you confirm in what capacity that was please?'

'I don't understand what you mean.'

'Well, were you having dinner in a professional capacity, to talk about museum visits, or in a more…social capacity?' clarified the detective sergeant.

'Socially, I guess. We had become good friends during the school trips.'

DCI Melrose looked across the room to where a

computer was sat on a desk. ‘Is that yours, Miss Da Silva?’

‘Yes. Well, no, not my personal one. It belongs to the school, but I use it on a daily basis.’

‘Does anyone else have access to this computer?’ asked DS Stanford.

‘The children can book time with it each day. And my teaching assistant. Why?’

DCI Melrose walked over and pushed the power button. ‘Do you mind if we take a quick look?’

‘Erm, I’m not really sure it’s a good time right now. I’m just a bit worried about the teaching assistant being on her own with the children. They can be a handful. Perhaps…’

‘It won’t take long,’ said DS Stanford, walking over to sit down in front of the computer screen.

Miss Da Silva turned pale as she watched the detectives. ‘I really think I should go and check on the class.’

‘Wait there, please,’ ordered DCI Melrose.

DS Stanford removed his mobile from his pocket and scrolled to the message from Cookie containing the instructions for finding the IP address of the machine. He read silently for a few seconds, before wiggling the mouse, to activate the sleeping screen. A few clicks later, he turned to DCI Melrose and showed her the IP address in Cookie’s text, before pointing at the IP address displayed on the computer.

DCI Melrose looked at Miss Da Silva, who was now perched on the edge of her desk, biting her nails. DS Stanford continued searching through the computer, uncovering the trail of emails that had been sent to Professor Hail. He opened the c: drive and found a folder labelled “MH”. When he double clicked on the icon to open the contents, a warning noise pinged and a pop-up box requesting a password appeared.

'Perhaps you know the password, Miss Da Silva?' said DS Stanford.

The teacher continued to bite her nails as she turned her head slightly, revealing the tears that had begun to gather in her eyes, and nodded nervously.

DCI Melrose gestured to the keyboard. 'If you wouldn't mind?'

Miss Da Silva sighed as she walked over to the computer. DS Stanford vacated the seat and guided her to sit down in front of the screen. From the chair, she looked up timidly at the detectives, her hands poised above the keyboard, her fingers reluctant to type.

'Either you unlock this folder for us, or we'll have the computer seized and our digital forensics team will open it instead and then I'll charge you with obstruction,' said DCI Melrose.

Miss Da Silva turned back to the monitor and began to enter her password. Upon completion, the folder opened revealing a collection of videos and photos, all labelled with a date, time and location.

'It's not what you think,' said Laura, cradling her head in her hands and sobbing. 'I loved Malcolm. I would never have harmed him.'

'Did you send Professor Hail threatening emails?' asked DCI Melrose.

'All the time we spent together, he never realised I was completely infatuated with him. He was smart and handsome and so passionate about his work. Soon I was making excuses to go to the museum. I'd end up walking around the galleries like a giddy teenager, hoping that I would bump into Malcolm. I tried dropping hints. Even after having dinner, he still didn't get it. It was frustrating how blind he was to my feelings. Next thing I knew, I had setup an anonymous email account and was sending messages to Malcolm.'

'Where did you go after leaving the exhibition on Saturday night, Miss Da Silva?' said DS Stanford.

'I went home. I left the museum around half eight, got home just before nine.'

'Is there anyone that can confirm that?' said DCI Melrose.

'My housemate. I stayed up talking and drinking with them until around 2am.'

'Write down their details here, please,' said DS Stanford, handing over his notebook and pen.

Laura scribbled a name and phone number, before passing the pad back. 'Am I in trouble?'

'We'll need to verify your alibi first,' said DCI Melrose. 'Can you tell me what all these videos and photos are, please?'

'When I wasn't getting anywhere with Malcolm, I decided to follow him. I know it's pathetic, but just being near him was the next best thing to being with him. It gave me an opportunity to learn more about him, to gather information I could use to get closer to him.'

DS Stanford beckoned to DCI Melrose to follow him to the other side of the room, until they were out of earshot.

'What are you thinking, Jack?'

'If Laura had been following him, this footage may give us an insight into the days leading up to his death. It's a long shot, but…'

'It's a good idea. Let's make the arrangements to have the PC taken back to the station. We can add it to DC North's viewing list.'

DCI Melrose walked back across to the computer. ‘Miss Da Silva, can you think of anything in this footage that might be of immediate interest to us and the murder inquiry?’

Laura ran her fingers across the mouse, hesitating for a moment, as she considered the request.

‘Yes, there is something that may help. There was…an incident…last Tuesday.’

‘What happened?’ asked DCI Melrose.

Laura nodded at the screen and clicked the play button.

Together, they watched as the footage started to load on the screen. They could see Professor Hail sat at a table in a café, talking to a woman opposite him. She was positioned with her back to the camera and the left side of her body was partially covered by a square pillar.

‘Any idea who this is?’ said DS Stanford, tapping the screen.

‘No, sorry. I followed Malcolm to the café and she was already waiting for him. She doesn’t turn around at any point.’

‘Have you ever seen him meeting her before?’ said DCI Melrose.

‘No, this was the first time. I’ve seen him in the café before, but usually he’ll grab a coffee to go.’

DS Stanford moved his face closer to the screen. ‘Can we enhance this in anyway? Or zoom in at all?’

Laura tried a few settings, before conceding that it wasn’t possible, not without the quality of the video deteriorating.

‘He doesn’t look very happy,’ observed DCI Melrose.

‘No, he wasn’t. Look at this next bit,’ said Laura.

The three watched as Professor Hail stood up and

leaned across towards the unidentified woman, saying something angrily, before swiping a cup off the table and storming out.

Laura clicked a button and the video stopped.

'What happened next?' said DCI Melrose.

'I left and went home. I didn't see the point in hanging around anymore and I didn't want Malcolm to bump into me when he was so angry. I've never seen him like that. His face was bright red with anger when he left the café.'

'Is this the one down the far end of the high street, near to the library?' said DS Stanford.

Laura nodded. 'That's the one.'

DS Stanford turned to DCI Melrose. 'I've been there a few times and definitely seen CCTV cameras in the corner.'

'It's worth a shot. Even if they don't have any footage, perhaps one of the serving staff will have heard something from the conversation. Let's stop by there on our way back to the station.'

DCI Melrose's phone began to ring. She excused herself and left the room, before answering the call and bringing the handset up to her ear.

'DCI Melrose here.'

'It's DC North. Just letting you know that I've finally got my hands on the museum footage from the security company. I'm just about to start trawling through it now, but thought you might want to know.'

'Thank you, DC North. We're just about to leave the school and head back to the station, via a café in town.'

'Ah, perfect. I'll have a cappuccino, please. Oh, just one minute…Claire! Claire! They're doing a pit stop on the way back, do you fancy anything? Any sugar? No? OK. And a latte for DC Murphy as well, please.'

DCI Melrose rubbed her forehead in frustration. 'Right, we're not actually going there for refreshments. We're following up on a lead.'

'Excellent news. Although, since you'll be there anyway, perhaps you could still, you know, buy us the drinks…please?'

'If there's time, DC North. Well done on the footage. We should be back in an hour or so.'

DCI Melrose poked her head through the doorway. 'Thanks for your time, Miss Da Silva. We may be back if we have any further questions. In the meantime, one of our team will be along to collect the other files from you. Time to go, DS Stanford.'

17

'This is the closest we'll be able to get parked,' said DS Stanford, pulling up the handbrake and unbuckling his seat belt.

DCI Melrose peered out through the passenger seat window. 'Whereabouts is this café?'

'Just along that side road there, about 100 metres down.'

'OK, let's get going. I want to get back to the station as soon as possible to see what progress DC North has made with the CCTV.'

The car alarm bleeped twice as they walked away from the vehicle, in the direction of the café.

'Not a lot of chain stores along here,' observed DCI Melrose.

'Not down this one, no. The main town centre is made up of two streets, both running alongside each other. This one has all the independent shops and the other one has the chains.'

'Sounds like a good setup,' said DCI Melrose. 'Wherever possible, I always tried to shop with the stand-alone retailers back in London.'

DS Stanford pointed up at a sign in the shape of a coffee cup. 'Here we are. That looks like the table they were using, so judging from the angle of the footage, Miss Da Silva must have been stood over there, behind those railings.'

DCI Melrose pulled open the door, a small bell chiming to announce their arrival. Inside, the smell of coffee beans and pastries filled the air and there were several groups of people huddled around, most of them deep in conversation.

The detectives snaked through the arrangement of tables and chairs and headed up to the front counter, where a blonde waitress wearing a blue apron was wiping down the marble surface.

'What can I get you?'

'We just have a few questions,' said DCI Melrose, showing her badge.

The waitress gestured to the detectives to follow her towards the other end of the counter, where they could have more privacy. 'How can I help?'

'Were you working here last Tuesday?' said DCI Melrose.

The waitress nodded.

'There was a man and a woman sat at that table. After knocking a cup onto the floor, the man stormed out of the café. Do you remember that happening?'

The waitress nodded again.

'Do you know what happened?'

'The woman came in first, ordered a tea and sat down. Then about five minutes later, the man arrived. He didn't order anything. He just walked in and headed straight over to the table.'

DS Stanford looked up from his notebook. 'Have you seen either of them in here before?'

'Yes. The man has been here before, perhaps every other week he pops in. Usually orders a coffee to go. I don't think I've seen the woman before, but then again, she was wearing quite large dark sunglasses.'

'Did you overhear what they were discussing?' asked DCI Melrose.

'Not to begin with. There were quite a few other people in that day, so I was either serving up here or clearing the tables. But, when he stood up to leave, it caused quite a commotion and everyone went quiet. I heard him lean across and say, "I know what you've done. It's over." Then he smacked the cup onto the floor and left. The woman wasn't far behind, leaving me here to clean up the blooming mess.'

DCI Melrose looked up into the corner of the room. 'Do you still have the recording from the camera for that day?'

'We should do. But that camera only takes still images, every 30 seconds. We didn't see the point of investing a lot of money in a fancy, complicated system. We're just a small café. We don't usually get much trouble. I can print off some of the stills from the time they were here. Or I could chuck some onto a CD for you. I've probably got a blank disc somewhere in the office.'

'The disc would be great, thank you,' said DCI Melrose.

'Give me a few minutes.'

The waitress disappeared through a doorway behind the counter as DCI Melrose turned to survey the groups of customers. 'Popular place, isn't it?'

'Yes, it's nearly always the busiest café on the high street. Their pastries are the best in town.'

'That reminds me – DCs North and Murphy put in a request for some drinks. Let's grab a few treats to take back with us as well, keep the morale up.'

'Sounds good to me.'

A few minutes later, the waitress returned and handed a CD across to DCI Melrose, secured in a plastic case.

'Here you are, Detective.'

‘That’s really helpful, thank you.’

‘Is there anything else I can help with?’

‘Actually, yes. We’d like to place an order to go, please.’

18

'Special delivery!' announced DS Stanford, almost skipping into the investigation room, carrying an assortment of pastries and drinks.

DCI Melrose followed closely behind. 'DC Murphy? Would you mind running this disc down to Cookie, please. Ask her to enhance the images and bring them here as soon as she can. Thank you.'

'Right away,' said DC Murphy, taking hold of the CD and hurrying away.

'Wait, one second!' called DS Stanford, stopping the young constable just as she reached the doorway.

'Yes, DS Stanford?'

'Here…take one of these down to her. They're her favourite. And, it might help persuade her to prioritise the photographs.'

DCI Melrose laughed. 'Should we be bribing staff?'

'I see it more as incentivising,' smiled DS Stanford.

'Less talk, more tea…please,' said DC North.

DS Stanford handed over a cup. 'You ordered a coffee.'

'Yes, but I didn't think "less talk, more coffee" was as snappy.'

DC North reached across to take one of the jam-filled pastries before retreating back to his desk.

Within seconds, he had devoured every last bite and was sweeping his desk for crumbs as DCI Melrose walked over and stood next to him.

'How are you getting on with the footage?'

'Well,' said DC North, pausing to take a sip from his cup, 'I've managed to make quite a bit of progress.'

DC Murphy walked back onto the floor. 'Cookie said she'll need an hour or so.'

DCI Melrose nodded. 'Thanks. You and DS Stanford had better join me here. DC North is about to take us through the CCTV from the museum. When you're ready, Detective Constable.'

'The security company gave us access to the footage from the Thursday, Friday and Saturday, in case the murderer did a pre-visit. I started with the footage on the balcony and as I forwarded my way through, I noticed that the angle of the shot slowly began moving. In real time, the adjustment is so slight that the guards wouldn't have noticed it, particularly as they work shifts. In total, I would say it turns about two metres to the left of where it was originally positioned.'

'Someone was moving the camera bit by bit in the days leading up to the murder, but only slightly each time, so that it wouldn't be picked up in the control room?' asked DS Stanford.

'Exactly,' answered DC North.

'And I'm guessing those two metres are enough to stop us from seeing the murder being committed?' said DCI Melrose.

'Unfortunately, yes,' replied DC North. 'This also means we still can't say for sure if it was an inside or outside job either. The camera on that floor could easily be accessed by staff and visitors. No other camera covers that area.'

'Over what length of time is the camera being moved?' asked DC Murphy.

'The movement begins on Thursday afternoon and is completed by late Friday. I'd say about 24 hours in total, but with a gap overnight.'

'And what about the guard, Max? Can we prove that he was sleeping?' said DS Stanford.

'The camera in the office is setup to capture the central section of the room, where the guard would sit to monitor the CCTV consoles. You can only see a corner of the sofa on the opposite side of the room and you can't see the door at all. There isn't anything suspicious about the positioning angle – I checked with the security company and this is how it has always been. From the footage I've reviewed, Max begins his shift sat in front of the screens, then leaves every hour for a routine patrol. The last time he returns in full view of the security camera is at 11:30 p.m. But he doesn't return to the chair; instead, he walks over to pick up his mug from the control station and then moves across towards the sofa area out of shot. We don't see Max again until 5:45 a.m., when he reappears, stretching and yawning.'

'Since the door is next to the sofa, we have no way of knowing whether Max left the room after we see him at 11:30 p.m.,' said DCI Melrose. 'Good work, DC North. Review the footage once more, please, just in case anything was missed the first time around. Let's all carry on.'

One by one, they returned to their desks, with DCI Melrose pausing briefly at the investigation board to add the details from that day so far.

'Do we bring Max Roberts in?' said DS Stanford.

'It's all circumstantial at the moment,' said DCI

Melrose. 'The CCTV doesn't prove, or disprove, anything. We need something more concrete.'

'I might be able to help with that,' said DC Murphy. 'I've just been sent Mr Roberts' bank statements. Guess what? Until recently, he was mostly in his overdraft, but then there were cash deposits of £1000 paid in on five different dates. I've cross-checked them and the deposits were made around the same time as the burglaries. And the final deposit was made on the Saturday of the exhibition opening. Just before Professor Hail was killed.'

'That's good enough for me,' said DCI Melrose. 'You and DC North collect him from his house and bring him here, please.'

***

Max sat nervously in one of the interview rooms. His hands felt cold, but he couldn't manage to rub them together. The nerves were getting the better of him. He looked at his reflection in the glass opposite. His face was wrinkled; his body withered. Time had ravaged him. The door swung open with a bang and DCI Melrose entered carrying a file full of paper. DS Stanford appeared shortly after and closed the door behind him.

'Mr Roberts, do you understand why you're here?' said DCI Melrose.

'Not really, but I'm guessing it has something to do with the professor's murder?'

'That's correct. And, just for the record, do you also understand that you are entitled to legal representation, but that you have chosen to waive this right?'

'Yes, that's right. I've done nothing wrong.'

‘Can you take us through the night of the murder?’ said DCI Melrose.

‘You’ve already asked me about that.’

‘And I’m asking again. What happened?’

‘I did my last walk around at 11:30 p.m., then I fell asleep until the morning. I woke just before 6am and raised the alarm. Look, you know all this, I don’t see the point of going through it again.’

‘The CCTV shows you entering the security office at 11:30 p.m., but then we don’t see you again until close to 5:45 a.m. How do you explain that?’

‘Because I was sleeping.’

‘Now that we’ve seen the footage, we only have your word for that, Mr Roberts. In our initial interview, you said you were picking up extra shifts due to money problems.’

‘Yes, what about it?’

‘Well, we’ve just reviewed your bank statements and it seems your financial worries have been eased somewhat by a series of £1000 deposits. What can you tell me about them?’

Max said nothing. His hands were beginning to ache.

‘Mr Roberts, I’ll ask you again. Where did the money come from?’

‘OK, OK. A few weeks ago, I was leaving work when I was approached in the car park by someone wearing a mask.’

‘A mask?’ said DS Stanford.

‘Yes, of an Egyptian mummy. They gave me an envelope containing £1000 and told me to make sure I left the museum unattended for a six-hour window during my night shift later that week. They said if I did what they asked and kept my mouth shut then I would have the opportunity to earn more. I was desperate for the cash, so I stupidly agreed. Whenever they wanted me out of the way, they would leave an envelope of cash under my wiper, with the date and times I had to be out.'

'And you didn't put two and two together to link this to the burglaries?' said DS Stanford.

'The museum is insured so they could easily claim back the money for any losses. It seemed like a victimless crime.'

'What about the night Professor Hail was killed? What were your instructions?' said DCI Melrose.

'I had to be out by midnight and then return by 5:45am. That way I would be seen at the beginning and end of my shift, so no one would be suspicious.'

'And when you found the body?'

'I panicked! I knew how the bribes would look, so I came up with the story about falling asleep.'

'How do we know you're telling the truth now?' said DS Stanford.

'You've seen my accounts. How else would I have got that money? Besides, I had no reason to kill Professor Hail.'

DCI Melrose and DS Stanford stepped out of the interview room and sighed simultaneously.

'Well, that was unexpected,' said DS Stanford. 'Whoever paid that money has to be behind the burglaries and the murder. What do we do with him now?'

'At the moment we don't have enough to arrest him for murder. Our best option is to charge him with perverting the course of justice and accepting a bribe, then release him on bail. If he is more involved than he's letting on, I want to see what he does next.'

'I'll speak with the custody sergeant.'

***

'The snaps are in!' declared Cookie, as she ran into the investigation room waving a brown envelope above her head.

'Bring them over here, please,' said DCI Melrose, walking over to a table behind her.

Cookie hurried across, tussling DS Stanford's hair on her way through, before handing the batch of pictures over.

'DS Stanford, you had better join us as well, please,' said DCI Melrose, as she switched on a low hanging light. She placed the glossy photos next to each other on the surface of the table. From a drawer, she brought out a square magnifying glass and began scanning slowly from left to right.

'This is the best we can enhance them?' said DCI Melrose.

'Afraid so,' replied Cookie. 'The quality wasn't that great to begin with. Enlarging a poor-quality photo just results in a pixelated mess.'

DS Stanford looked over their shoulders. 'You can't see her face properly in any of these. It's almost as if she knew where the camera was!'

'Maybe we don't need to see her face to identify her,' said DCI Melrose, tapping one of the pictures.

'What am I looking at?' said DS Stanford.

DCI Melrose lifted the photograph off of the table and handed it to her colleague, along with the magnifying glass. 'Look at the left wrist.'

'A bracelet?'

'Yes, a bracelet I've seen before.'

'Where?'

'In a photo at Ms Browning's house.'

'So, this is Professor Hail's ex-wife?'

‘No. I have reason to believe that this is Miss Westbrook.’

‘The collections co-ordinator from the museum?’

‘Indeed.’

Cookie looked back and forth as this exchange took place, moving her head from side to side as if she was observing a tennis match. ‘Do you need anything else?’

‘No, that’s all for now,’ confirmed DCI Melrose. ‘Thank you, Cookie, this has been incredibly helpful.’

‘Great. I’ll be back down in the tech cave if anyone needs me.’

DCI Melrose turned to face DS Stanford. ‘Looks like we’re taking another trip, I’m afraid. We have a few questions to ask the glamorous Miss Westbrook.’

19

'It looks as though a murder hasn't kept the visitors away,' said DS Stanford, surveying the lengthy queue outside the main door as they pulled into the museum car park.

'Sadly, it has probably attracted more people,' said DCI Melrose. 'Considering we only allowed the museum to partially reopen late yesterday afternoon, they haven't taken long getting the crowds back through the doors.'

'Word spreads fast in this town. I'm sure we'll have a bunch of amateur investigators inside, all following up on their own theories.'

As they walked towards the museum entrance, several people in the waiting crowd recognised them and began to call out.

'Is the murderer still on the loose?'

'Why haven't you made an arrest yet?'

DCI Melrose and DS Stanford offered no response and continued up the steps. As they arrived in the entrance hall, they caught the eye of Edith Chapman, who was stood on the far side of the room, speaking to a young couple. She quickly excused herself and walked over to meet them.

'Good afternoon to you both.'

'Hello again, Mrs Chapman. I see the crowds are back,' said DCI Melrose.

'Yes, the exhibition has been popular, but many of these people are also well-wishers coming to pay their tributes. We've had to allocate an area in one of our quieter galleries for all the flowers and cards that people have brought in. There's also a book of condolence, which is filling up fast. He really did mean a lot to this town. How can I help you? Do you need to ask more questions about what we spoke about this morning? I probably have an email trail in my archives that confirm what I told you.'

'No, thank you, Mrs Chapman. We're actually looking to talk to Miss Westbrook. Is she in today?'

'Georgie? Erm, yes, yes, I'm sure I've seen her somewhere. Let me put out an announcement for her.'

'That would be great, thank you.'

Edith scurried away in the direction of the security office, glancing over her shoulder every couple of steps to look back at DCI Melrose and DS Stanford. Within a few seconds of her disappearing into the side room, the speakers came alive with her voice.

'Staff announcement: please can Georgie Westbrook make her way to the main entrance. That's Georgie Westbrook to the main entrance, please. Thank you.'

As they waited, DCI Melrose and DS Stanford watched as the stream of visitors made their way through the security checks at the front and then funnelled along to the "Finding Fossils" exhibition.

Some of them were carrying donations for Professor Hail's ever-growing shrine, but many were there simply to take a look at the artefacts before they were packed up and sent off to the next stop on the tour. Life was already beginning to move on.

Edith returned from making her announcement. 'She won't be long, I'm sure. No doubt she's checking on the space for another new exhibition that we're hosting in two weeks.'

'I had no idea museum work was so busy,' said DCI Melrose.

'Oh, yes! There is always lots going on behind the scenes. A museum is like an iceberg. The part above water is what you see all around you here: the artefacts, the paintings, the museum itself. Below the surface, you have everything else: the archives, the storage of artefacts no longer fit for public viewing, the planning, sourcing the materials, liaising with other museums both in this country and across the world. The list goes on.'

'Well, you learn something every day,' said DCI Melrose.

'The metaphor could apply to an investigation as well,' remarked DS Stanford. 'Always lots going on below the surface.'

'I can imagine,' said Edith, looking around to see if Miss Westbrook was nearby. 'Ah, here she is.'

Georgie appeared through a doorway just to the left of the staircase and headed across to where the trio were stood. 'What's going on, Edith? Have you some news for us, DCI Melrose?'

'We would just like to ask you a few questions, if that's OK?'

'Of course. Shall we go along to my office?'

'That would be ideal, thank you.'

'Do you need me to join you?' said Edith.

'No, just Miss Westbrook. Don't let us take up anymore of your time, Mrs Chapman.'

'Well, you know where I am if you need anything else,' said Edith, before walking to the other side of the room, all the while keeping her attention on the three of them.

DCI Melrose turned back to face Georgie. 'Shall we?'

'Please, follow me. My office is only a short walk away.'

They began making their way across the Great Hall, walking past the entrance to "Finding Fossils".

'It's proving to be popular then?' said DS Stanford, weaving through the line of people.

'Yes, the response has been very positive so far. If only Professor Hail were here to…um, well, he would have been extremely proud.'

She wiped a tear from the corner of her eye.

'I'm sure,' said DCI Melrose. 'It must have taken a lot of work to bring it all together.'

'More late nights than I care to remember. It's always worth it in the end though. Although I can't say I always enjoy the journey! Would you like anything to drink? We're just about to pass a staff kitchen on the way, so I can quickly grab some tea or coffee.'

'Not for me, thank you,' said DCI Melrose.

DS Stanford shook his head. 'I'm fine, thank you.'

'If you change your mind I can always run back out, it's no trouble. Well, here we are. Please, step inside.'

The room was compact, with barely enough room for the three of them. Most of the space was taken up by a desk and chair, which were both squeezed up against a tiny window and a small bookcase. Georgie moved a pile of books from a foot stool, before flipping a plastic crate on its end and brushing the dirt off the top with her hand.

'Sorry, I don't usually have visitors in here. I can go and find some better chairs, if you would like?'

'No, honestly, these will be fine, thank you,' said

DCI Melrose, carefully sitting down on the footstool. DS Stanford walked across to the crate and pushed down on it a few times to test its strength, before eventually lowering himself onto the edge.

Georgie chuckled nervously. 'So, how can I help?'

DCI Melrose removed a photograph from her pocket and slid it across the table. 'Is this you, Miss Westbrook?'

Georgie prised the picture from the wooden surface and studied it for a few seconds, before looking back at DCI Melrose.

'Yes, this is me.'

'Can you let me know what this meeting with Professor Hail was about?'

'I bumped into him there, that's all. I was waiting for someone else and Malcolm had popped in for his regular takeaway coffee. When he saw me, he decided to join me for a few minutes and we talked about the museum.'

DS Stanford shuffled on the crate, trying to find a more comfortable position to sit. The creaking of the plastic filled the silence for a few seconds.

DCI Melrose flipped over a page in her notebook. 'Miss Westbrook, a witness overheard Professor Hail saying, "I know what you've done. It's over." Can you explain what Malcolm was referring to please?'

Georgie stood up from her desk and turned to look through the window, placing her left palm against the glass. DCI Melrose was about to repeat the question, when Georgie suddenly burst into tears. The two detectives looked at one another, both surprised by her reaction.

Georgie turned back to face them, taking a tissue out of one of the desk drawers and wiping the tears away from her eyes. 'I'm so sorry.'

'Miss Westbrook, what was the meeting really about?' said DCI Melrose.

'Malcolm was breaking up with me.' She let out a pained shriek as she began sobbing again.

'Are you saying that you and Professor Hail were in a relationship?' asked DS Stanford.

'Yes. We'd been together for a few months.'

'Why didn't you mention this before?' said DCI Melrose.

'No one at the museum knew. Malcolm said it would be better to keep it a secret. Particularly with him in line to replace Edith. I'm really sorry. I know I should have said something.'

'Can you explain what Professor Hail meant by, "I know what you've done", Miss Westbrook?' said DS Stanford.

Georgie dabbed her eyes and sat back down. 'I was at a conference about 2 weeks ago, giving a speech on inter-museum collection transfers. During the networking sessions, the organisers were taking photos and one of them happened to be with my arm around one of the other delegates. A man. There was nothing in it at all, we'd only met earlier that day. We were just posing for a photo. I swear, it was completely innocent.'

'But Professor Hail didn't sec it that way, I'm guessing?' said DS Stanford.

'He saw the photo on the conference website and went ballistic. I tried to explain, but he wouldn't listen. It all sounds like silly teenage stuff when you say it out loud.'

'What was the name of the conference? And the website?' said DCI Melrose.

Georgie jotted down the details on a notepad and tore the page out of the book before handing it across.

‘Thank you,’ said DCI Melrose, folding the paper in half and sliding it into her pocket. ‘Is there anything else that you haven’t told us, Miss Westbrook?’

‘That’s everything. Honestly. I’m sorry I didn’t say anything before, but I’m sure you can appreciate the awkward situation I found myself in. I was worried it could affect my place here at the museum. And I didn’t think it was important, we hadn’t been together long, it’s not like we were in love.’

‘Let us decide what’s important,’ said DCI Melrose, standing up. ‘Thank you for your time, Miss Westbrook.’

‘Of course. Thank you, detectives.’

Kate and Jack left the room and began walking back to the museum entrance.

‘Well. That was…yeah, awkward,’ said DS Stanford.

‘Indeed. They’d obviously done a good job at keeping it quiet around here. We’ll get DC North to check out the website and see if he can find this photograph.’

‘Do you think it could have been her that murdered Professor Hail then?’

‘The jilted lover? Possibly. But if they’d only been together for a couple of months, it does seem a bit of an extreme reaction. Ugh, I think I might need to have a late-night session.’

‘Drinking?’

DCI Melrose laughed. ‘Not quite. I meant an evening at the station, reviewing all the evidence, going back over alibis. Searching for the missing piece of the puzzle that will help to complete the picture.’

‘Sounds like a good idea to me. Do you like

Chinese takeaway? I know a good place.'

'Now you're talking!'

DCI Melrose and DS Stanford weaved back through the crowded hall, eventually arriving at the main door. They exited the building, unaware that Edith was still stood, observing their every move. Once they had disappeared from sight, she hurried along the corridor in the direction of Georgie's office.

20

'This is quite a spread, DS Stanford! Excellent work.'

DCI Melrose was pacing the break room, surveying the numerous silver trays of food laid out upon the table.

'I wasn't sure what you'd like, so it gave me the perfect excuse to order most of the menu,' said DS Stanford. 'I'm sure DC North and DC Murphy won't mind helping us out.'

'Not me, boss,' said DC North, entering the room. 'I've got plans this evening. Er, if that's alright, DCI Melrose?'

'Of course. No sense in all of us staying here. Where's DC Murphy?'

'She's just changing. I think I overheard her talking to her boyfriend about meeting up in town for dinner tonight.'

'Well, DS Stanford, it seems only the two of us will be tackling this mountain of delicious food. I hope you don't mind being stuck here with me.'

Jack laughed. 'I'm sure I'll survive. We can put the leftovers in the fridge for lunch tomorrow.'

'Yes, please!' said DC North. 'Oh, by the way. I checked out that website you gave me and there is a picture of Georgie Westbrook with another man. They do look pretty cosy, but it doesn't say who he is though.'

'Thank you, DC North,' said DCI Melrose. 'I hope you have a good evening.'

'You too. See you both in the morning.'

DCI Melrose turned to DS Stanford, handing him a knife and fork. 'Let's load up the plates and head back to the investigation board and run through the case from top to bottom.'

DC Murphy was walking through the main office in a figure-hugging red dress as the detectives returned from the kitchen with their dinner.

'Lovely dress, DC Murphy,' said DCI Melrose. 'That colour really suits you.'

The young detective constable blushed. 'Thank you. I'm meeting my boyfriend in town for dinner. It's our anniversary today. You don't mind, do you?'

'Of course not! And congratulations to you both. How long have you been together?'

'It's three years this evening. We're going back to the place we went on our first date.'

'How romantic. I hope you both have a great evening.'

'Thank you. Oh, by the way, Alice Browning's alibi checked out. Her parents emailed photos of her at an 80th birthday meal over two hours away. They confirmed it didn't end until 2 a.m. and she stayed the night. I've also been through Professor Hail's bank records. He withdrew £5000 a few weeks ago.'

DS Stanford coughed as he choked on a piece of food. 'Ugh. Sorry. Went down the wrong way. Five thousand pounds?'

'Yes, it was quite unusual activity for him. Looking at his spending patterns, the Professor was very thrifty with his money. I've emailed the full details across to you both.'

‘Could be related to the money that Max received. Excellent work, DC Murphy, thank you,’ said DCI Melrose. ‘You’d better go or else you’ll be late. Have a good evening and we’ll see you in the morning.’

Claire smiled, before wrapping a knee-length coat around her shoulders and leaving the office.

‘Right then. Let’s start from the beginning, shall we?’ said DCI Melrose, putting her plate down on her desk and walking across to the investigation board. DS Stanford brushed his hands together and wiped his face with a napkin, before joining her.

DS Stanford tapped a photo stuck on the centre of the board. ‘Professor Hail, found impaled on a dinosaur skeleton at 6 a.m. on Saturday. Discovered by this man here, Max Roberts. He originally claimed he was asleep at the time of the murder, but we’ve since discovered he was bribed to leave the museum during his shift.’

DCI Melrose moved across and pointed to another photo. ‘Alice Browning, ex-wife of the victim. Inherits his estate, including £500,000. However, her parents have confirmed that she was with them at the time of the murder. Alice has also said that the money will be used to fund a new wing at the museum.’

‘Next, we have Professor Stone. The victim was just about to publish a book that would have discredited Stone professionally. Not only did Stone know the layout of the museum, being a former employee, but we caught him sneaking back into the victim’s office to return a stolen proof copy of the new book. His neighbours did say that they saw him arrive home Saturday night and didn’t see him leave until the following morning.’

‘Then there’s Edith Chapman. The victim was replacing her as the director of the museum, but she claims to have known this already and even recommended him. The taxi company confirmed dropping her home, but since she is widowed, there is no other way of confirming that she remained there for the rest of the night.'

DS Stanford walked back to his desk and picked up a spring roll, which he crammed into his mouth as he returned to the front of the room.

'Georgie Westbrook,' said DS Stanford, in between chewing. 'The restaurant she went to have said that they saw her with a group of friends, but she left at midnight, not 1 a.m. like Georgie told us. We now know that she was in a relationship with the victim, which ended shortly before his murder.'

'Which brings us to our last suspect, Laura Da Silva, the primary school teacher and over enthusiastic admirer. She sent the victim threatening messages and was stalking him. But her roommate confirmed that she was at home during the time of the murder.'

DCI Melrose tapped the marker pen against her chin. 'Let's also start making a list of the other mysteries surrounding the case in this corner here.'

'Top of that has to be William Carter. We still don't know why the victim had a passport and birth certificate containing his photo and that name.'

'Then there's the unidentified woman that Professor Stone saw walking out of the victim's office.'

'Yes, and our newest mystery is the money that Professor Hail withdrew,' said DS Stanford. 'Perhaps he had something to do with the break-ins? He could have been stealing from the museum with a partner and they double crossed him?'

DCI Melrose wrote the figure of £5000 on the

board and circled it, adding a question mark at the end. They both stepped back and looked over the notes and pictures.

'OK, next steps,' said DCI Melrose. 'I'll update DI Swift about the bribes and see if that ties in with any of his findings.'

'I'll take a look at the finances of the other suspects and compare them with Professor Hail's and Max's. If we can follow the trail, it may lead us to the murderer.'

The detectives sat down at their desks, alternating between typing on their computers, flicking through paperwork and eating the takeaway. Every 30 minutes or so they would both make a trip to the kitchen to top up their drinks and replenish their food supplies. A few hours passed by and when DCI Melrose leant back in her chair to rub her eyes, the hands on the wall clock were pointing to 11:30 p.m.

'Time really does fly when you're having fun,' she laughed.

'I think the food helps! Did you have many late-night takeaway sessions back in London?'

'A few,' smiled DCI Melrose, reminiscing in her mind. 'We had quite a good selection of outlets not far from the station.'

'That's the beauty of London, I suppose.'

'Yes. It had its disadvantages as well. How long have you been in Spiral Bay?'

'All my life. I was born just down the road at the local hospital. Went to the primary and secondary schools here, then signed up for the force when I realised that teaching History wasn't for me.'

'How lucky you were to grow up by the sea.'

'The views are pretty breath taking and I love living here, but it isn't always smooth sailing. Yes, pun intended.'

DCI Melrose chuckled. ‘How come?’

‘The main problem with being a seaside town, is that you have a seaside economy. We’re inundated with holidaymakers during the summer months, but then we empty out around autumn and winter. It makes it hard for some businesses to survive, particularly if we have a crap summer. I’m lucky that my job provides me with a salary all year round.’

‘I can imagine. I guess you never really think about that when you go on holiday to places like this. They must rely on their summer takings to get through the quieter periods.’

‘Yes, some places will even close for a month or so when there are less people around.’

‘Are your family from around here as well?’

‘My dad first came over from Jamaica with my granddad in the seventies. He was only a small boy. They’d been sold a dream, basically. Told they could have a better life here. I’m not sure it ever materialised for my granddad, but he never gave up searching. They moved around to begin with, but ended up here in the mid-80s. That’s when my dad met my mum and started “courting”, as the old timers call it. Next thing they knew, mum was pregnant with my sister, Connie. They quickly got married, my mum gave birth and then a year later, she was pregnant with me.’

‘Where are they all now? If you don’t mind me asking, of course.’

‘Granddad passed away a few years ago and went to join my grandma in the stars. Mum and dad live up the hill. Nice bungalow, overlooking the sea. Connie has a flat near me with her husband, Sam and my nephew, Bailey.’

'Sorry to hear about your granddad. I'm glad that you still have the rest of your family nearby though. I haven't had too many chances to sit and feel alone yet, but I know that when this case is over and I'm sat on a day off, I'll realise how much I'm going to miss my family down here.'

'Well, whenever you start to think that way, give me a call. There's always plenty of things to do here to take your mind off it.'

'Thanks, Jack. Don't get me wrong, I'm grateful to be here. I'm glad I got this job.'

'Me too. And, so are a lot of people. DC North in particular.'

'DC North. Really?'

'Imagine what his life would be like if DI Swift had taken over.'

DCI Melrose laughed. 'Point taken. Anyway, we should probably call it a night there. Thank you for your company and, more importantly, for the takeaway. I'll put the rest in the fridge before I go home, so that they can enjoy the leftovers for lunch.'

'Or breakfast, knowing DC North! I think it's been a very productive evening.'

'Absolutely, I agree. We've tidied up a lot of the loose threads and I'm sure tomorrow we'll gain more ground, coming at the case refreshed.'

21

The air was cold as I stepped out of the office at around midnight. I didn't want Jack to have to go out of his way to drop me home, so I had ordered a taxi. The lights along the promenade looked so picturesque in the dark, like twinkling guardians of the night.

Sat in the back of the car, I realised this was the first moment I'd had for personal reflection in the last 18 hours. I've always found it useful to have these periods of calm, where you filter out the bad and soak up the good. Cleansing the day, I suppose.

I was grateful that my health had been good that day. Sounds silly, doesn't it? But when you're living with a chronic illness, even the smallest window of normality can feel like the biggest victory. Enjoy the highs, because the peaks aren't forever. It doesn't take long before you're slipping down the other side of that hill.

The case is frustrating the hell out of me. I have always liked puzzles, but that doesn't mean I'm a fan of puzzles I can't solve. As the new detective in any town, solving the first crime assigned to you is key to building local confidence. I left my good reputation behind in London; one that I had spent years building. I'm a nobody here.

As the taxi turned into my road, I shuffled forward slightly. 'If you could just pull over here on the left, that would be great, thank you.'

I stepped out of the car and handed a ten-pound note through the window, telling the driver to keep the change. She thanked me, before driving off along the road and out of sight around a corner.

The houses on both sides were sat in darkness. Out of nowhere I felt a tingle rush down my spine. Not from the cold, but from some deep rooted, policing instinct. I've had it for years. When it happens, I know something isn't right. And at that moment, I knew I was being watched.

I waited for a second, slowly looking around. The streetlights had cast murky shadows intermittently along the road where cars were parked, straddling the pavement. I put my hand in my pocket to search for my house keys, before starting to walk the ten or so steps to the end of my driveway.

'Miaow!'

Suddenly, out of a bush, leapt Chester, rolling into a ball and ending up at my feet. I stumbled back slightly, grabbing onto the pole of a parking sign to steady myself.

'Shit!'

I tried to whisper the word, but it left my mouth as more of a hiss.

'What are you doing out here?'

I picked Chester up and cradled him in my arms, rubbing his belly as he waved his paws about in the air. Then I turned the question over again in my mind.

'What are you doing out here?'

There was no cat flap on the house. There were no windows left open during the day. Perhaps Rachel let you out? Or maybe you somehow escaped in the morning when I left for work?

I crept up the driveway trying not to make a noise,

still carrying Chester like a new-born in my arms. As I edged nearer to the porch, my heart skipped a beat. The door was slightly open. Fragments of wood and metal were discarded on the step, from where I assumed a crowbar had been used to prise the lock from the frame.

My instinct was to rush in and search from room to room to see if the bastards were still inside the house. But I'm also human and fear isn't automatically removed during police training. I quickly retreated back down the driveway and called the station.

'This is DCI Melrose, calling from outside my home. There's been a break in. Send a patrol car out here as quick as you can, please.'

With the phone secured in my pocket I carefully walked back up the driveway, until I was stood behind my car. I pushed the fob button and slowly opened the back door on the driver's side, just wide enough to allow me to tilt my arms and encourage Chester onto the seat. With the cat safely inside, I closed the door gently and moved around to open the boot.

Keeping my eyes on the front door, I felt through the contents of the rear compartment until I clutched what I recognised to be a torch. I switched this into my other hand and continued feeling around until I had located the backup baton I always kept in my car. With the boot closed and the doors locked once again, I headed back to the front of the house.

The wooden shards on the step splintered into smaller pieces as I walked over them. I extended the baton and switched on the torch, the beam shining onto the door. I quickly raised it up to eye level, so that the cylindrical battery compartment rested upon my shoulder. I took a few deep breaths and then pushed the door open.

The hall and staircase looked empty. I moved slowly against the wall until I reached the doorway to the front room. I could feel my heart pounding faster and faster with every step. The silence of the house was deafening and I couldn't shake the feeling that someone was stood behind me, even though each time I checked I found myself alone.

I swept quickly into the living room.

Empty.

I pointed the torch in the direction of the kitchen.

Empty.

Perhaps they had already gone. Perhaps they had broken in, realised there was nothing worth stealing and left.

What was that?

A creak of a floorboard.

The noise had come from upstairs.

I took another deep breath and turned back to face the hallway and staircase. Come on, Kate; you can do this.

Step by step.

It's strange when it's your own place you're dealing with. If I was entering another property, I wouldn't be thinking twice like this. At least I knew that backup would be on the way and I'm only 15 minutes or so from the station. That's as long as there was a patrol car available. I tried to convince myself there would be.

I gingerly made my way back out to the bottom of the staircase and peered apprehensively down at the first step.

Here we go.

I strategically placed each foot, trying to remember where the looser parts of the boards were in order to minimise the noise. With each step, I moved closer to the top and closer to the unknown.

Bang!

The front door slammed shut, caught by a gust of wind. As I turned to look back down the stairs, I sensed someone walk up behind me from the first floor. Before I could react, a hand grabbed me around the back of my neck and sent me tumbling forward. The torch slipped out of my grip and spun in the air, before it crashed onto the hallway floor and the light went out.

I wasn't far behind and I landed with my head turned towards the front door. My vision began to blur. I threw my arms out, frantically reaching around for something to grip onto. I heard someone running down the stairs and was able to make out a rough outline of them as they jumped over my injured body before fleeing from the house.

In the darkness and with my eyesight affected, I couldn't identify any distinguishing features. My head was pounding and I couldn't fight the weight of my eyelids much longer.

Within a few seconds of the intruder escaping, I passed out.

22

'Kate! Kate! Are you OK?'

DS Stanford came rushing into the A&E cubicle in which Kate was resting on her side. She slowly opened her eyes and twisted her body until she was face to face with her colleague.

'Jack? What are you doing here?' Her voice was weary and strained.

'The station contacted me when the patrol car arrived at your house and found you unconscious.'

'What happened?'

'Officers are just going over the scene now, but it looks like you interrupted a burglary. The doctor tells me you have bruises on your neck, so we think you were grabbed from behind and pushed down the stairs.'

DCI Melrose slowly pulled herself upright, wincing as she moved her head. 'You normally have to drink to deserve a headache like this.'

'At least you've still got your sense of humour,' smiled Jack, placing his hand on her shoulder. 'Are you feeling well enough to go through a few questions?'

DCI Melrose nodded.

'What happened when you arrived home?'

'Erm. I remember feeling like I was being watched. And then…Chester. Oh no, Chester. Is

Chester OK? I think I left him in the car.'

'Yes, he's fine. Officers found him and they've taken him down the station to be looked after. What did you notice next?'

'The front door had been forced in. I grabbed a torch and my baton and went into the house. Oh, I called for backup first.'

'You should've waited until backup had arrived,' said DS Stanford, sternly.

DCI Melrose rolled her eyes, before cradling her head and scrunching up her face, overcome with pain.

'Just take it easy, Kate. You've had a nasty knock.'

Kate wedged a pillow behind her back and looked down at her arm. A drip was attached to a cannula in her hand. She followed the tubing with her eyes, up to the bags hanging from the drip stand.

'It's just some fluids and liquid paracetamol,' said DS Stanford.

'Yes. I'm familiar with them,' replied DCI Melrose, tilting her head away.

'Sorry. I didn't mean to patronise you.'

'No, that's not what I…never mind. What time is it?'

DS Stanford looked down at the watch wrapped around his wrist. 'It has just gone 4 a.m.'

'You should go home. We need to be on top form for the case.'

'I'm not going anywhere, Kate. Not until I know that you're safe.'

'Stubborn, aren't you?'

The conversation was interrupted by a phone call on DS Stanford's mobile. He retrieved it from his pocket and excused himself from the cubicle. DCI Melrose could hear him talking outside, although she struggled to make out any of the words he was saying. A few minutes later, he returned to her side.

'That was one of the officers at your house.'

'Oh? What did they say?'

'They've completed an initial sweep of the property. They can't see anything obvious missing. Upstairs in the bedroom, the intruder wrote a message on the wall: "Tread carefully, Detective Melrose".'

'A threat? It has to be related to the case.'

DS Stanford nodded. 'They've called out a team to fix up your door as well.'

'Thanks. Well, if we've rattled someone, it means we must be on the right tracks. Why else would they risk getting caught just to deliver a warning?'

'I just wish we knew what we had uncovered that triggered this.'

'Let's keep up the pressure. Let's keep doing what we're doing.'

'You can't come in to work today, surely?'

DCI Melrose could see the look of concern on DS Stanford's face. She placed her hand on his arm. 'I just need a few hours of sleep, then I'll be in. I'm fine, honestly. I imagine they'll discharge me soon.'

'OK. I'll head home then. Where will you go?'

'I'll stay in a hotel for a few nights. Just until I can get the house sorted. Thank you for being here, Jack. I appreciate your support.'

'I know you would have done the same for me. We're a team.'

DS Stanford waved as he backed out of the cubicle and walked away. DCI Melrose adjusted her body so that she was lying down once more, moving the pillow up to rest beneath her head.

For a while she watched the fluids trickle down the tubing and make their way along to her arm. The process was calming to observe, hypnotic even.

Despite the excruciating pain in her head and despite the hustle and bustle of the department, within a few minutes, DCI Melrose had managed to coax herself to sleep.

23

DC North and DC Murphy were both stood in the office whispering to one another when DS Stanford arrived at work.

'How is she?' said DC Murphy.

This was followed up quickly by DC North. 'What happened?'

'She's fine. Well, as good as can be expected. But, she's a tough cookie. Her house was broken into last night and she was attacked by the intruder.'

DC Murphy brought her hands up against her face. 'Oh, that's terrible.'

'Are we going to process the scene?' said DC North.

'No, there's a team there already from DI Swift's lot. They've been there most of the early hours.'

DC North let out an exaggerated sigh. 'You know as well as I do that Swift will bodge the investigation! He won't give a shit!'

'Regardless, it's their scene now. Any time that we spend on that is time lost on our case. Whoever did this is trying to scare DCI Melrose away. But that's not going to work, is it? We won't let them, will we?'

The detective constables shook their heads.

'Glad we're on the same page. Let's get on with the case. DCI Melrose and I reviewed the board last night and have added some more annotations, so familiarise yourself with them. Oh, and she is planning to come into work today. She won't want us to make a fuss, understand?'

The detective constables nodded.

'Great. Let's crack on then, please.'

DC Murphy disappeared into the kitchen, returning a few minutes later with a cup of coffee, which she placed on DS Stanford's desk.

'Thank you, Claire.'

'No problem.'

'Where's mine?' said DC North.

'You haven't been up all night, so you can make your own,' said DC Murphy, walking across to the investigation board.

'Well, that's nice, isn't it?' muttered DC North.

'Any more news about the £5000?' said DC Murphy.

DS Stanford looked up. 'Nothing yet.'

'Do you want me to go down to the bank? See if I can find anything out?'

'Perhaps give them a call to begin with. See if they remember anything unusual,' said DS Stanford.

DC North walked over to the board. 'Hang on. What's this about £5000?'

'Professor Hail withdrew that amount in the weeks leading up to his death,' said DC Murphy.

DC North rubbed the stubble on his chin. 'That's the exact amount of cash given to Max Roberts. There must be a link somewhere.'

'Or maybe he was in trouble. You know, being blackmailed?' said DC Murphy.

'Or, perhaps he just wanted to buy something extravagant,' said DC North.

'Wouldn't you just use a debit or credit card if you were buying something that expensive?' said DC

Murphy, before sticking her tongue out at her colleague.

DS Stanford left his desk and joined the detective constables at the board. 'It is a lot of money to be carrying around. We didn't find any amounts like that in his office or at his house and his wallet only contained his cards and ID.'

DC North suddenly jumped into the air, shouting: 'Giant Squid Storage!'

DS Stanford and DC Murphy stepped back in surprise, looking at one another, before turning to face their colleague.

'What did you say?' said DS Stanford.

'Giant Squid Storage. The Professor went there a few days before he died.'

'How do you know?' said DC Murphy.

'The pictures from the teacher. On one of the evenings that she was following him, he went to the Giant Squid Storage facility. The photos show him carrying a backpack in and out of the building.'

'You think a drop or swap of some kind took place?' said DC Murphy.

'It would make sense. We didn't find any record of Professor Hail renting any storage, so why else would he be there?'

'623,' said DS Stanford, rushing back to collect one of the files on his desk. 'On the envelope containing the passport and birth certificate it had the number 623.'

The trio were so engrossed by these developments that they hadn't noticed DCI Melrose enter the room and stand quietly listening to them.

'You think that could be the number of the container?' said DC North.

'It could be,' said DS Stanford. 'Maybe he

deposited the £5000 in the storage unit.'

'Why?' said DC Murphy.

The room went silent.

'Don't stop now, you're on a roll. Perhaps I should start later more often.'

'DCI Melrose!' said DS Stanford, turning to face her. 'We were just talking about the money.'

'I heard. Sounds like you might be on to something. DC Murphy, why don't you give the storage facility a call and ask them who box 623 belongs to?'

'Yes, straight away,' said DC Murphy. 'Oh, and I just wanted to say I'm sorry about what happened. I hope you're OK.'

'Me too,' said DC North. 'If you need anything, you know, just…look, don't make me get all soppy.'

DCI Melrose smiled and nodded, before heading over to her desk. DS Stanford walked across to join her.

'How are you feeling, Kate?'

'Better, thank you. And it honestly meant a lot that you came to the hospital.'

'No problem.'

The phone on DS Stanford's table began to ring. He smiled and nodded in the direction of DCI Melrose before rushing over to pick up the handset.

'DS Stanford here…OK…yes…and the fingerprints match? Great. Thank you.'

'What was that about?' said DCI Melrose.

'As the team were finishing at your house, they noticed a rectangular piece of metal on the floor just beneath the bed. It turned out to be a name badge. From the museum.'

'Who did the badge belong to?'

'Max Roberts, the security guard. They've

checked the prints and it's a match to the exclusion prints we took.'

'Right, let's get over to his house then.'

'They've already been. He's not there.'

'DC North, get on the phone to the museum. Find out if they've heard from him.'

The detective constable immediately picked up his phone and began dialling. 'On it, boss.'

DC Murphy rushed across the office. 'OK, so I've spoken to the storage company and guess who rented box 623?'

'Max Roberts?' said DCI Melrose.

'Max Roberts,' repeated DC Murphy.

DC North ended his phone call and joined DC Murphy. 'So, I just spoke with Edith at the museum and Max was due on shift tonight, but when she found out about his arrest, she suspended him. They haven't heard from him since.'

'So, once again, we've got nothing,' said DC Murphy.

'Get his photo and description out to all patrols – high priority,' said DCI Melrose.

As DC Murphy rushed back to her PC, the door to the investigation room burst open and DI Swift marched inside.

'Listen up! I thought you clowns would be interested to know that we're about to raid a house in connection with the stolen items from the museum.'

'Who does the house belong to?' said DC North.

'Gerald something or other.'

'That doesn't link with anyone we've come across in our investigation so far,' said DC North.

'Do I give a shit?' replied DI Swift. 'I'm not here to solve your bloody case as well.'

'Where's the address?' said DCI Melrose.

‘What am I? A bloody map? My team have the details, but it’s on Bay Avenue or Bay View Road, something like that. My team found the items listed on an auction site and followed the electronic trail.’

‘You didn’t use Cookie to track them back to the property?’ said DS Stanford.

‘I don’t need that techno geek. It’s not difficult.’

‘When were the items listed?’ said DCI Melrose.

‘Are we playing 20 questions or something? I don’t have time to stand around here explaining how real policing works. I’ll let you know more details when we’re back. Fuck me.’

DI Swift stormed out of the office, slamming the door behind him. Through the walls, they could hear him barking orders at his team as they shuffled along the corridor.

DC North scoffed. ‘He really is an absolute…’

DCI Melrose interjected before he could finish the sentence. ‘I’ll stop you there, DC North. He might be an absolute…but he is still a colleague and your superior. So, we’ll show him some respect, understand?’

‘Yes, boss,’ said DC North, like a puppy that had been scolded.

‘What’s the plan?’ said DS Stanford.

DCI Melrose sighed. ‘Not much else we can do at the moment except wait for any reports on the whereabouts of Max Roberts.’

‘What was the name of the road that DI Swift mentioned?’ said DS Stanford.

‘Bay View, I think. Why?’

DS Stanford rushed back to his desk and grabbed a file. He began to flick through the sheets of paper, before stopping on a page and following the words with his finger.

'Here! I thought I had heard a road name like that before, look.'

DCI Melrose walked over and leaned across his shoulder.

'The allotment!'

'But, how does this link in with the stolen items?' said DC North. 'He was paid to look the other way.'

'Double bluff,' said DCI Melrose. 'He was stealing the items himself and the deposits were from the profits he made selling the goods on.'

DS Stanford picked up his phone and dialled an internal extension.

'Cookie? It's Jackie. Could you pop up urgently, please?'

He replaced the handset and turned to DC Murphy.

'Can you go on the internet and find the auction site selling the stolen items from the museum please?'

DC Murphy nodded and turned to her PC.

'I have a feeling they've made a mistake on the trace,' said DS Stanford. 'But we'll need Cookie to verify that theory.'

'Do many allotments have internet access?' asked DCI Melrose.

'Not any that I know of. But don't you think it's too much of a coincidence that the items for sale have been traced back to an address next to the allotments used by Max?'

'OK, you have a point.'

Cookie walked into the room and made her way across to DS Stanford's desk.

'How are you feeling, DCI Melrose?' she said, her voice full of concern.

'Better. And thank you for asking.'

'I hope you catch the guy.'

'That's something you might be able to help us

with, Cookie,' said DS Stanford.

'How so?'

'DI Swift and his team are off on a raid of a house that they believe is linked to the stolen items from the museum.'

'OK. How does that link in with someone breaking into DCI Melrose's house?'

'We believe the person who broke in is a man called Max Roberts. He's the security guard at the museum. When we interviewed him, he mentioned that he had an allotment just off Bay View Road. The property that Swift is going to raid is on the same road.'

'Huh. That is quite a coincidence. What do you want me to do?'

'I think that DI Swift's team may have…made an error when tracing who uploaded the items on the auction site. Can you check for us, please?'

'I'll need the details of the auction site.'

DC Murphy looked up from her desk. 'I've found it. I'll email the details to you, Cookie.'

'Perfect, thanks. I'll head back downstairs and work my magic.'

'Thanks, Cookie,' said DCI Melrose. 'How long do you think it will take you?'

'Depends on the setup. But if DI Swift and his team have cracked it, I can't imagine it will take me too long. Perhaps twenty minutes, maybe less?'

'Give us a call as soon as you know, please,' said DS Stanford.

'No problem, Jackie. Speak soon.'

With that, Cookie hurried back downstairs. For a few minutes, the remaining occupants of the room sat in silence, looking at one another.

'Well, what do we do now then?' said DC North,

letting out a grunt of frustration.

'Not much we can do,' said DCI Melrose. 'We can't get in the way of DI Swift's raid until we know for certain from Cookie that they've made a mistake. We could jeopardise their entire investigation if we go storming in now without all the facts and to be honest, I don't think he'd listen to us anyway. Not without proof. DC Murphy, has there been any luck with the whereabouts of Max Roberts?'

Claire tapped on her keyboard. 'Nothing yet, no.'

'DS Stanford – I think you and I should take a drive out to Max Roberts' house and see what we can find for ourselves.'

'No problem, I'll bring the car out the front so you don't have to walk too far.'

DCI Melrose glanced at DS Stanford with raised eyebrows. 'I think I can manage the short distance to the underground car park, thank you.'

'No, I know. I just thought that…'

Before DS Stanford could finish, his landline began to ring.

'Lucky! Saved by the bell,' joked DC North.

DS Stanford glared in Joseph's direction before lifting the handset to his ear.

'DS Stanford. Cookie? Well, that was quick! Hang on, let me put you on speaker phone…OK, go ahead.'

The team gathered around the phone as Cookie began to speak.

'OK, so it didn't take long to trace this and you're right – DI Swift and his team have made a big mistake. They've traced the router rather than the actual device. It's a piggybacking scenario.'

'A piggy what?' said DS Stanford.

'The wi-fi router at the address that they're going to raid is unsecured.'

'Meaning anyone could access it?' said DCI Melrose.

'Yes, within a certain range. I followed the trace beyond the router and it led to a handheld device, looks like a mobile phone.'

'What sort of range are we talking about?' said DS Stanford.

'It depends on the strength of the signal. But with the power of the routers nowadays, especially ones with a booster, it's possible that the wi-fi could have been accessed from as far away as 60 metres or so.'

'Which means that Max Roberts could have been using the wi-fi from a device in his allotment,' said DCI Melrose.

'That's correct. I'm 100% certain that the auction site wasn't accessed from the property DI Swift and his team are going to.'

'Thanks, Cookie. We'll talk later,' said DS Stanford before hanging up the phone.

DCI Melrose smashed her hand on the table. 'That stupid, arrogant fool!'

Her reaction caught the rest of the team by surprise.

'Yes, I know I said we should respect our colleagues, but what an absolute idiot! OK, you two – get me a printout of the allotment layout, identifying the plot belonging to Max, then get your gear and get out there. I know there's a small chance that someone else is accessing the wi-fi of that property, but it feels like too much of a coincidence to me. Perhaps Max has a shed there or something and has been using it to store the stolen items. DS Stanford and I will follow and I'll get in contact with DI Swift. We need to stop him and his team from making a big mistake.'

24

The silence down Bay View Road was broken by the sound of screeching tires as the two police cars sped between the rows of houses and out onto a small dirt track leading to allotments at the end.

They pulled to a stop on a large square section of gravel that acted as a car park, alongside DI Swift and his team, who had diverted to the allotment following the phone call from DCI Melrose. The mixture of armed response officers, police constables and detectives quickly congregated around DCI Melrose, who was unfolding a map of the allotment on the bonnet of one of the cars.

'Boss,' said DC North, 'that's Max Roberts' car over there.'

'OK, listen up everyone. I want the perimeter secured. There are potential exit points here, here, here and here. We need someone on each of those. This square here is the shed and that's what we are going to breach. If you look above this hedge to that tree over there, around 50 metres away, the shed is just beyond that. According to this diagram, the shed is approximately 6ft by 8ft, with a door here and no windows. Max Roberts is suspected of murder, attacking a police detective and stealing from the museum. We don't know what sort of reception we're going to get, so stay focussed. According to Cookie, the electronic device that has been accessing the nearby wi-fi was last active 15 minutes ago. OK, let's move!'

The group quietly split off. One team of officers swept out wider to protect the boundary and the rest hurried along in a tight formation as they made their way towards the shed. As the inner group approached the wooden hut, they spread out to form a circle around the structure. DCI Melrose and DS Stanford positioned themselves just outside the main door, followed closely by DI Swift.

DCI Melrose looked around at the team to check everyone was ready before calling out. 'Max Roberts! This is the police. We have you surrounded. Please step out of the shed, with your hands held out in front of you.'

There was silence. DCI Melrose glanced across to DS Stanford, who nodded in acknowledgement and moved towards the side of the doorway and reached for the latch. DI Swift moved in closer, his gun cradled in his hands. DCI Melrose counted down from three with her fingers and on the final signal, DS Stanford pulled the door open and DI Swift rushed into the shed.

'He's dead!'

DCI Melrose and DS Stanford advanced to the doorway and looked inside. Without any windows, the interior was dark, but they could both see Max Roberts slumped over in a wicker chair with a gunshot wound to his head. On the floor, just beyond the reach of his left hand, was a gun.

Blood had been sprayed up the wall next to the body and a further pool had formed on the floor. DI Swift checked for a pulse, but this only confirmed his initial assessment. DS Stanford pointed across to a stack of crates.

'That looks like a collection of the stolen items from the museum.'

DI Swift moved across and inspected them. 'Yep. This is them. And look, there's a note pinned to the wall here.'

DCI Melrose shone a torch in the direction of the paper. 'What does it say?'

DI Swift leaned closer and began to read. '"I'm sorry for everything I've done. I didn't mean for anyone to get hurt. I hope you can forgive me. Max."'

'OK, you'd better step out now, DI Swift, so we can preserve the scene. DS Stanford, we need to get a tight perimeter set up around here and I want all the allotments sealed off. There's going to be quite a bit of activity and that's going to generate a lot of public interest – place some officers at each entrance to reduce the chance of the area being contaminated. Get the SOCOs out asap and call the medical examiner. Ask DC Murphy to arrange for family liaison to contact the next of kin and get DC North to co-ordinate door to door enquiries. Someone may have seen Max arriving or heard the sound of the gunshot.'

'I'm on it,' said DS Stanford, pulling his mobile phone from his pocket.

'Looks like we'll be closing both our cases today then,' said DI Swift, holstering his handgun.

'Hmm, that's how it looks, doesn't it?'

DI Swift could sense the coldness in her tone. 'Look, I know we got off to a rocky start. But I wanted to say thanks for making the call to me. You could've let me make a fool of myself.'

DCI Melrose nodded and headed back to the car park. DS Stanford was sat on one of the bonnets just finishing a phone call.

'The team are on their way, should be ten minutes or so. The FME on call today is Dr Shaftesbury again. He's heading over, but he's currently stuck on the other side of town so he will probably take a bit longer.'

'Thank you. I want to take a look around Max's home, but we'll need to get the landlord to let us in. Can you get in touch with him, please?'

'Of course. What about the crime scene?'

'DI Swift can take the lead on this one in my temporary absence, since he is the reason that we came out here in the first place. But I want you to stay here and oversee the operation from our side, please, until I return. I'll go to Max's house, have a quick look around, then head back here. I shouldn't be more than an hour or so.'

'Oh, OK. Yeah, of course, no problem. Let me give the landlord a call. Won't take a minute.'

'Thanks, Jack. I'll go and let DI Swift know.'

As DCI Melrose walked back towards the shed, DS Stanford searched through his emails until he found the details of the landlord. He copied the phone number onto his clipboard and pasted them into the call screen. The ringing tone looped around several times before there was any answer.

'Hello?'

'Hello, this is DS Stanford, calling from the Spiral Bay Police force. I understand you currently let a property to Mr Max Roberts, is that correct?'

'Yes, that's correct. What's happened?'

'We need access to the property immediately. Please can you be there to meet my colleague, DCI Kate Melrose, within the next 15 minutes?'

'Yes, I will head over now. Can you tell me what this is all about?'

‘DCI Melrose will explain everything in person. Thank you for your assistance.’

25

The drive to Max's house only took ten minutes and by the time I arrived, the landlord was already waiting for me outside.

'Thank you for being here at such short notice,' I said, reaching out to shake his hand. 'My name is Detective Chief Inspector Kate Melrose and here's my identification.'

'Thanks. My name is Jerry. Your colleague on the phone was quite vague about the reason for the urgency to get inside.'

'Yes, I'm sure you're wondering what this is all about. There's no easy way to say this, but I'm sorry to have to tell you that Mr Roberts has just been found dead, at his allotment.'

The landlord sat down on the garden wall and stared ahead. For a while he didn't say anything. Every person I've ever delivered this type of news to has always reacted in a different way and it takes time to process.

I stood quietly beside him with my hands nestled into my pockets. The sun was beginning to break through the clouds and I could feel a gentle breeze across my cheeks. At any other time, this would have felt like a window of peaceful tranquillity worth savouring. Somewhere, someone would be enjoying this moment. After a few more minutes of silence,

Jerry looked up towards me.

'How did he die?'

'I'm really sorry but I can't release any details at the moment. How long had he been renting from you?'

'Oh, must be coming up to 10 years or so now, I imagine.'

'Have you ever had any issues with him?'

Jerry let out a short burst of laughter.

'With Max? He is one of my best tenants. Always pays his rent. Keeps the place clean.'

'When did you last see or speak to him?'

'A few days ago. One of his drains was blocked so I popped over to take a look.'

'How did he seem?'

'He was really shaken up about that body he found, you know, at the museum. The dead professor. He's had it bad enough recently, what with all the break-ins there as well.'

'He spoke to you about them?'

'Not in any detail. You know, small talk, I guess.'

'OK, thank you, Jerry. If it's OK, I'd like to take a look inside please, alone.'

'Er, yeah, of course. I'll, er…I'll wait here for you then.'

Jerry dropped the keys into my hand and resumed his previous position, staring into nothing.

'Thanks, I won't be long.'

I've seen a lot of dead bodies during my time on the force. I don't think I'll ever be numb to the experience, but I have found mechanisms to cope. I wouldn't say that I'm an overly religious person, but one thing I do is to think of the dead bodies as vehicles and nothing more. A simple mode of transport. The real person isn't something physical that you can touch, like flesh and bones. Their essence is more ethereal than that. And once the vehicle is no longer fit for purpose, it breaks down and is left behind. But the person inside, the real person, moves on. Without that belief, what am I left with? The thought that when someone dies, that's it. They return to the soil and their life is merely a blip on the Earth's timeline.

The part I'll never get used to is going through the victim's belongings and all the material possessions left behind. Sifting through the life of another. Despite being a means to an end, it always felt intrusive. The process often reminded me of my own health struggles and in a way magnified the delicate fragility of my own mortality.

If bodies were a vehicle, then mine would have failed every MOT. I've always wondered who might end up going through my life, when I trade for a newer model.

As I stepped inside the hallway, I noticed that the air was musty, as if the windows hadn't been opened for a few days. I pulled on a pair of protective gloves and shut the door behind me. The stairs stretched up to my left and straight ahead an open doorway led to the kitchen. There was a closed door on the right-hand side, opposite a cupboard beneath the stairs, so I decided to look in there first.

The door creaked as I pushed it open, revealing a dark sitting room. Most of the daylight was being blocked by a closed pair of thick, grey curtains. I flicked the light switch next to me and a bulb hanging down from the middle of the patterned ceiling stuttered on.

The only seat was a small armchair, facing a television set in the far corner. On the wall opposite me, were rows and rows of books all neatly lined in an oak bookcase. I noticed that they had been ordered alphabetically by the surname of each author. Other than that, there wasn't much else to see.

I popped my head through the kitchen doorway and took a quick scan. There was nothing out of the ordinary: a cooker, microwave, kettle, toaster and two mugs placed upside down on the draining board. I headed back towards the front door and began climbing the stairs.

The first floor consisted of a double bedroom, a box room full of old music records and a bathroom. There was no sign of any stolen items from the museum. Perhaps Max had decided that keeping them at his house would have been too much of a risk. Better to store them down the allotment, where people might not think to check.

I stepped into the bathroom and opened the window to look outside. The back garden was nothing more than a small, rectangular patch of grass, with a collapsed rotary washing line in the middle. I noticed how quiet it was. I couldn't hear any traffic. I couldn't hear any people.

I watched as a small robin flew across from a bird feeder in the neighbour's garden and landed on one of the wooden fences. For a while it sat there, twitching its wings, before flying away again.

I stepped back from the window and turned my focus to a small cabinet just above the sink. I pulled the mirrored door towards me, the latch clicking as the panel swung open. My eye was immediately drawn to a box of tablets. I lifted them out and read the label: Methotrexate. Take once a week. Dose: 20mg.

My grip weakened and the packet dropped into the

ceramic sink, sliding back and forth for a couple of seconds before resting over the plughole. My vision began to blur. I placed my hands down to steady myself. Suddenly, I felt as if I couldn't breathe. I gasped, struggling to take in any air. I was overcome with dizziness as I fell to my knees on the bathmat. I fought as much as I could, but I knew how this panic attack would end. The same way it always ended. With a flashback.

***

'I can't do it!'

I screamed as loud as I could, fighting against the tears that were beginning to trickle down my cheeks.

'They said this might help you, sweetheart,' said my dad, in his diplomatic way. 'Control your UC, perhaps?'

'Kate, you need to try. Please.'

My mum was sat on the end of my bed, pleading with me. I looked down at the syringe of methotrexate in my hand. I looked back at my mum. She didn't say anything else. She didn't need to. I could tell what she was thinking by the look on her face. My dad stood by the window. His expression was full of his usual optimism.

I tore open a paper sachet and removed an antibacterial wipe. I lifted one side of my shorts up, exposing my left thigh and began to wipe the skin, cleansing the area. I paused again.

My mum placed her hand on my shoulder and I looked across at her and smiled. Not a beaming, happy smile with all my teeth on display. No. It was a meek, timid, smile. One that disappeared almost as quickly as it had emerged. The smile of a terrified little girl in a woman's body.

I carefully removed the safety guard covering the needle and placed it on a small tray on my duvet. I closed my eyes for a few seconds and took in some deep breaths.

OK.

This is it.

This might make you better.

I moved the needle down towards my leg and pinched a small section of the skin between my fingers. I rested the tip on my thigh and waited. It felt as if I sat like that for an eternity. In truth, it was only a matter of seconds. Courage overcame me and I pushed the top of the needle, puncturing the skin and waited until all the liquid had gone.

'Well done, Kate. I know that wasn't easy for you.'

My mum was rubbing my arm in encouragement. I placed my hand over hers and raised another half-hearted smile. At least it was done now. Until next week. And this whole episode would be repeated again.

***

A shrill ringing noise cut through the scene and I quickly opened my eyes. The bathroom window at Max's was still open and a soft breeze was blowing through. I reached for my phone and sat up against the bathtub.

'Hello?'

'Kate? It's DS Stanford. Are you OK?'

'Yes, why?'

'You've been gone a while, that's all. Dr Shaftesbury has finished with the body and they're

just taking Mr Roberts away. Forensics are working on the shed at the moment, but I don't think they'll be much longer. Are you heading back soon?'

'No, it sounds like you've got everything under control there. How about I meet you back at the station in an hour?'

'No problem. See you then.'

I dropped the phone back into my pocket and sat there for a few more minutes, letting the gentle touch of the wind calm me. The flashbacks had been happening for a few years now. I hadn't yet worked out how to control them as they would often come out of nowhere, triggered by the slightest memory. A type of PTSD, I suppose.

I placed my hand on my left thigh. The skin had recovered now, but I could still remember the pain of the bruising, caused by the injections. But I would do anything to keep my UC under control. That determination hadn't changed. Ultimately, I knew that surgery was likely to be the only answer. Until then, I'm stuck in a cycle of being fine one day, then in hospital the next. Or collapsed on the bathroom floor in a victim's house, recovering from another panic attack.

How much longer can you do this to yourself, Kate?

How many more times does this need to happen before you get help?

These are the recurring questions I can't face answering right now.

Snap out of it, Kate.

You're stronger than this.

You're a survivor.

26

‘DI Swift is already out there in front of the press, patting himself on the back for recovering the stolen items,’ said DC North, peering out into the main reception from the investigation room. ‘Look at him. Waving an antique vase around like he’s won the World Cup.’

‘He hasn’t mentioned the fact that we found Max Roberts dead as well, has he?’ said DS Stanford.

‘No, of course not,’ replied DC North, returning to his desk. ‘That would take the attention away from his victory and he wouldn’t want that.’

‘If it wasn’t for us, he would’ve been stood there apologising for raiding an innocent man’s house,’ said DC Murphy.

‘Now, I would have paid to see that,’ laughed DC North.

‘Good evening, everyone,’ said DCI Melrose, walking in through the side entrance.

‘Did you find anything interesting at the house?’ said DS Stanford.

‘Not really. He had a supply of methotrexate, but I don’t know if he was taking them. That’s about all I learnt. I didn’t even find any other stolen items. He must have stored them all at his allotment. Let’s get the team out to his house, in case I’ve missed anything.’

'Dr Shaftesbury is carrying out the autopsy later today, so we should have the full results by tomorrow at the latest.'

'Excellent, thank you.'

'What do we think then, boss?' said DC North. 'Here's my theory: Max stole the goods, was caught red-handed by the prof so he killed him. Then, when he was overcome with guilt decided to off himself.'

'Very eloquently put,' said DCI Melrose, dryly. 'That's certainly the way it seems, isn't it? There is a possibility that Professor Hail was in on it. The £1000 could have been Max's share of the sales, but then he got greedy and decided he wanted it all for himself.'

'If they were both making money though, surely there would be deposits in Professor Hail's account and the only activity of significance is the £5000 withdrawal,' said DC Murphy.

'Very true,' said DCI Melrose. 'How did you get on with your door-to-door enquiries?'

'No one heard a gunshot,' said DC North. 'But a few people did identify Max from his photo as a regular user of the allotment. The general impression was that he seemed friendly and approachable. They saw him talking with some of the other plot owners on occasion. Nothing ground breaking really.'

'No one heard a gunshot?' said DS Stanford.

'Perhaps being in the shed masked some of the noise,' said DC North. 'And his patch is set quite far back from the houses. By the way, I've put a copy of the suicide note on the board.'

The group left their desks and gathered around as DS Stanford read the words out loud:

'"I'm sorry for everything I've done. I didn't mean for anyone to get hurt. I hope you can forgive me. Max."'

The phone on DS Stanford's desk began to ring.

'DS Stanford here. Cookie, hi. Right. OK. No, that's great. Thanks. Yeah, speak soon.'

'What did she want?' said DCI Melrose.

'So, she has been digging around the mobile phone from the scene and it was definitely the device used to list the stolen items.'

'OK, that's a good start,' said DC North.

At that moment DI Swift entered the room and walked over towards them.

'Off you go then, London copper. That lot out there want a statement from you. About the dead body you just found. I've warmed them up for you.'

'What did you tell them?' said DCI Melrose.

Before he could answer, DI Swift had already walked back out of the door, laughing to himself.

'What are you going to say?' said DS Stanford.

'That we've found a dead body and are in the process of investigating any links to the murder at the museum. Look, it's been another long day today. Let's come at this fresh in the morning. We should have the autopsy by then as well. I'll go and deal with the media.'

'Do you want any support?' said DS Stanford.

'No, honestly, it's fine. I'll go home after this. Thank you though. Oh, and DC North? Can you stop by the Giant Squid storage facility tomorrow please on your way in and see if box 623 has anything in it?'

'Consider it done, boss.'

'Thanks. OK, well, have a nice evening everyone. I'll see you all tomorrow.'

DCI Melrose made her way through the office to the main entrance. She paused just inside the room and took a deep breath. As she pushed the door open, the group of reporters scrambled into position, holding their recorders out in front of them. DCI Melrose blinked as flashes of light filled the foyer.

'Good evening, my name is DCI Melrose and I'm the senior investigating officer on the Professor Hail case. I'm here to make a statement about further developments that have occurred this afternoon. We found the body of Max Roberts, one of the night guards at the museum, at an allotment off Bay View Road. I can't release any further details, but we are investigating the link between this death and the murder of Professor Hail.'

Flash. Flash. Flash.

Another round of photographs.

The group began to scuffle amongst themselves, trying to get closer to DCI Melrose, who had stumbled back slightly during the melee.

'I'm sorry but I won't be taking any questions at this time.'

Kate retreated into the empty investigation office and dropped down on the carpet, her back propped against the door. She remained there for a while, hugging her knees to her chest, using every ounce of strength she had left in her to fight away the tiredness, frustration and tears.

27

'Good morning,' said DCI Melrose, entering the investigation room, waving a paper bag.

'What have you got there?' said DC Murphy.

'Pain au chocolates,' said DCI Melrose, placing them down on a desk in the middle of the room. 'Help yourselves.'

DS Stanford and DC Murphy quickly made their way across and opened the bag eagerly, both thanking DCI Melrose in the process.

'Where's DC North?' said DCI Melrose.

'He's stopping by the storage unit,' said DS Stanford.

'Of course. Any news on the autopsy?'

'Should be coming through in the next few hours.'

'Excellent.'

DS Stanford grabbed a newspaper from his desk and walked over to Kate.

'I don't suppose you've seen the front pages this morning, have you?'

'No, why?'

DS Stanford unfolded the paper and handed it across.

'Really?' said DCI Melrose, scanning the article. 'Oh, pur-lease! "Swift Success with Stolen Items" – there wasn't anything quick about it, the case has been going on for weeks! I bet he is absolutely loving this though. Look at that picture of him. Oh well, tomorrow's chip paper, I guess?'

'Exactly. We've got Max for the burglaries, all we have to do now is prove that he killed Professor Hail, then we'll be able to wrap our case up as well.'

'I never thought that my first case here would be so frustrating,' said DCI Melrose.

'Yeah, it's not been a straightforward one, has it?' laughed DS Stanford.

'The biggest joke of all is that when I told my old team where I was going, they all said I'd be back within a month to escape the boredom.'

'You city slickers always underestimate us out of town folk, don't you?' said DS Stanford, smiling.

'I had the Chief Superintendent on the phone earlier. He's getting heat from the media now and he wanted reassurances that we were going to catch our killer. Seems my holding statement yesterday didn't do enough to placate them.'

'What did you say to the Chief Superintendent then?'

'Not much I could say. It doesn't look good though, does it? I'm a green DCI, in a new town and I have two dead bodies on my hands.'

'You might not yet have the experience of a Detective Chief Inspector, but you've got plenty of years behind you on the force. You're still the same person. Other than the title, what's really changed?'

'Accountability.'

'We're a team. We're all accountable.'

DCI Melrose smiled.

'Thanks, Jack. I'm glad I've got a good team around me. Do you fancy a quick trip out?'

'Yes, of course. Where did you have in mind?'

'I thought we could take another look around

Professor Hail's office. See if it sparks anything.'

***

The detectives walked up the steps to the museum entrance and stepped inside. There were fewer visitors around today than there had been on previous occasions. A group of schoolchildren were bunched up in the Great Hall, trying to listen to the instructions from their teacher. Kate and Jack bypassed them all and headed straight up the steps and along the corridor to the office.

'Is there anything in particular you're looking for?' said DS Stanford.

'Nope. Just have a scan. See if there's anything that makes sense now given what we know about this case. Something that might not have jumped out at us before.'

The two detectives spent the next twenty minutes searching the room, covering every inch. DS Stanford looked under the desk again, where he had previously found the passport and birth certificate. There was nothing he had missed during his initial search. DCI Melrose lifted every book in the room by its cover and fanned the pages out, checking for any other hidden documents. Nothing.

'OK, maybe this was a stupid idea after all. I don't think we're going to find anything else,' said DCI Melrose.

'I have another suggestion that might sound a bit silly, if that would make you feel any better?' said DS Stanford.

'Go on.'

'Well, every time we've been to the museum, it's been with a purpose. We've been for interviews, or for CCTV, or to look at the crime scene. Why don't we just visit the actual museum itself? This is where Professor Hail worked and died. These are the people he mingled with on a daily basis. We need to take a look into his world. Perhaps that might spark something?'

'Doesn't sound like a silly suggestion to me. Besides, it might help us to clear our minds. Where shall we start?'

'How about "Finding Fossils"? I've always fancied myself as a bit of a dinosaur hunter.'

'Well, you're in the perfect location, you know, living on the Jurassic coast. Lead the way.'

DCI Melrose and DS Stanford left the office and made their way back down the stairs and across the Great Hall towards the entrance of the exhibition.

'DCI Melrose? DS Stanford?'

The detectives turned around to find Edith Chapman walking over to them.

'Mrs Chapman, how are you?' said DCI Melrose.

'Not too good, as I'm sure you can understand. It's awful about Max. To think that he was the one stealing from the museum and that he felt his only way out was to kill himself. I wish he'd come to me if he was in financial difficulties.'

The trio walked through an archway into one of the galleries and sat down on a bench beneath a large painting of a man.

'How did you know it was suicide?' said DCI Melrose.

'Oh, well, I just assumed. Er, DI Swift was here earlier and he briefed me on both cases. Yes, he said about you finding Max at his allotment. And the suicide note. And the stolen items.'

'DI Swift? Right, I see,' said DCI Melrose. 'Mrs

Chapman, were you aware of any medical conditions that Max had?'

'Medical conditions? No. As far as I knew, he was fit and healthy. For his age, anyway. Why?'

'No reason, thank you,' said DCI Melrose.

'Have all the staff been told about Max?' said DS Stanford.

'Not everyone. We've let the guards know, obviously, because they all worked so closely together. And I've let Georgie know too. She had a bit of a soft spot for him. They used to have lunch together whenever he was on a day shift. I think she saw him as a bit of a father figure at work.'

There was a brief lull in the conversation and DCI Melrose took the opportunity to stand up and scan the paintings in the room. Her eyes eventually fell on the picture that was hanging behind the bench.

'That looks familiar,' said DCI Melrose. 'It's like the one of Professor Hail in his office. Same pose, same background. Who's the man in this painting?'

'Oh, that's Howard Carter,' said Edith, twisting to look behind her.

'As in the archaeologist? The one who discovered Tutankhamun's tomb?' said DS Stanford.

'That's the one,' said Edith.

DCI Melrose moved closer. 'I don't believe it! Look! The plaque!'

'Painting of Howard Carter,' said DS Stanford. 'Painted by his brother…William Carter.'

'Of course!' said Edith. 'I don't know why I didn't think of that when you asked me before.'

'How is this painting related to the murder?' said DS Stanford.

'I don't think it's *this* painting that's related,' said DCI Melrose. 'I think the link is the artist and subject.

The painting in the office was signed by someone with the initial 'M' and the surname 'Hail'. Do you know who that could be?'

'That's Mark. He's Malcolm's brother,' said Edith. 'He painted that recently at Professor Hail's request. Howard Carter was a bit of a hero to him, so I think it was a tribute of sorts.'

'That's it!' said DCI Melrose.

Without warning, she went rushing out of the room, trailed by DS Stanford who was running behind, trying to keep up with her. By the time he arrived at the office, slightly out of breath, DCI Melrose had already taken the painting from the wall and was ripping the back off. As she did so, a small memory card slipped out and dropped onto the floor.

'This could be the breakthrough we need,' said DCI Melrose, picking the card up off the floor. 'Let's get this back to the station and see what's on it.'

28

'DC Murphy, run this down to Cookie urgently, please,' said DCI Melrose, walking into the investigation room alongside DS Stanford.

'And tell her that Jackie wants this treated as a priority,' said DS Stanford. 'We'll be down in a few minutes for an update on what she's found.'

DC Murphy acknowledged their request as she rushed out of the door. DCI Melrose walked behind her desk and put her bag in the bottom drawer, before joining DS Stanford by the investigation board.

'How did we miss that on our searches?' said DS Stanford.

'There was paper covering the back of the frame and the card was hidden inside,' said DCI Melrose. 'There wouldn't have been any obvious reason to tear it open at the time.'

'Cookie is already making a start,' said DC Murphy, panting as she returned to her desk.

'DS Stanford, let's head downstairs then,' said DCI Melrose.

They quickly left the investigation room and made their way down to the basement, eager to see what the tech genius had uncovered so far.

'Come in, come in,' said Cookie, as they opened the door.

'What have you got for us?' said DS Stanford.

‘Well, Jackie, the professor had password protected the card, but thankfully it didn’t take too long to get through that. There’s only one folder, called “Evidence”.’

‘That’s what he was accessing on his PC,’ said DCI Melrose. ‘What’s in the folder?’

‘A few photos, a list of items and prices, a map of the world with dates and times written next to various countries and a flier for a courier company.’

‘Go to the photos first,’ said DS Stanford.

Cookie opened the first thumbnail and began scrolling through.

‘They look like items from the museum, that’s all,’ said DCI Melrose.

‘Wait! That’s the storage unit,’ said DS Stanford. ‘And look, he’s taken a photo of the inside of 623. That’s the envelope we found underneath his desk.’

‘Show me the price list please, Cookie,’ said DCI Melrose.

‘No problem. Here you go.’

‘Look! Passports from all different countries and prices for each one,’ said DCI Melrose.

‘Birth certificates, driving licences, you name it,’ said DS Stanford. ‘Guns and drugs as well.’

‘We found a passport and birth certificate, didn’t we?’ said DCI Melrose. ‘Add the prices of those two items together from this list.’

‘Five thousand pounds,’ said DS Stanford.

‘Exactly!’ said DCI Melrose.

‘Cookie, can you run an internet search for the courier company?’ said DS Stanford.

‘Anything for my Jackie. It’ll just take a few clicks…OK…here ya go.’

‘Keep scrolling. Keep scrolling. There. Click on the “About” section please.’

‘No problem.’

‘Aha!’ said DS Stanford. ‘Look who they list as one of their customers.’

‘Yes, it’s falling into place now,’ said DCI Melrose. ‘What about the map of the world with the dates and times?’

‘Here you go,’ said Cookie.

‘Look at the last date on the list,’ said DCI Melrose.

‘That’s today,’ said DS Stanford.

‘Exactly,’ said DCI Melrose. ‘And look at the time. Eight o’clock this evening. That’s good work, Cookie, thank you. Come on, DS Stanford, let’s get back upstairs.’

***

‘I still don’t understand the link between the passport and the birth certificate,’ said DC Murphy, as DCI Melrose and DS Stanford returned to their desks.

‘We’re a bit ahead of that now,’ said DS Stanford.

Before he could elaborate further, the office phone began to ring.

‘DC Murphy speaking. Of course, I’ll get her for you. It’s Dr Shaftesbury, he wants to discuss the autopsy results before sending them across.’

‘Thanks, put him through please. Hello, Dr Shaftesbury. Yep. OK…Hang on, let me put you on speakerphone so the team can hear this. One second…OK, you’re on speaker now, can you repeat what you just told me please?’

‘The cause of death was the gunshot wound to the head, no surprises there. But this is where it gets interesting. He was taking methotrexate, I found

evidence of the drug in his bloodstream.'

'That's quite a heavy drug to be on,' said DS Stanford. 'That's used for cancer patients, isn't it?'

'Among other things,' said DCI Melrose, before backtracking slightly. 'Erm, I think, anyway. Is that right, doctor?'

'Correct. There are a few other groups of patients that would take this drug.'

'What was he taking it for?' said DS Stanford.

'Rheumatoid arthritis.'

'Meaning what exactly?' said DCI Melrose.

'I found evidence that when he died, Mr Roberts had been experiencing quite an extreme flare-up. In my professional opinion, there's no way he could have fired that gun or written the suicide letter.'

'When do you think the flare-up began?' said DCI Melrose.

'Difficult to say with any certainty, but I'd estimate that it will have been at least a week.'

'Would you say it's unlikely he could have picked up the vase that hit Professor Hail or pushed him over the ledge?' said DS Stanford.

'Yes. I would say both of those would be extremely difficult during a flare-up.'

'Do you have a time of death?' said DCI Melrose.

'It would have been within a one hour window, prior to you finding him.'

'Thank you for your call, Dr Shaftesbury, that's been really helpful.'

'No problem. I'll send over the official report shortly. Speak soon.'

'Those results mean it is more likely that Max was used as a scapegoat,' said DCI Melrose. 'Which also suggests he didn't break into my house or steal from the museum either. If he's been struggling with his hands, there's no way he could have lifted all those items out.'

'Unless there actually was a partner,' said DC Murphy.

'And Professor Hail was on to them both and so the partner killed him,' said DS Stanford. 'Then they got greedy and killed Max.'

'Based on the evidence we've seen on the memory card, it's possible,' said DCI Melrose.

'Who wants to tell DI Swift?' said DS Stanford, barely concealing his amusement at the thought of the pompous Detective Inspector being wrong.

'He'll get the autopsy results,' said DCI Melrose. 'He can make his own conclusions from that.'

'He's never reopened a case before, I don't think he'll start with this one,' said DC Murphy.

'That's not our problem right now,' said DCI Melrose. 'We need to work out who is really behind all this.'

DC North came striding through the door.

'I might be able to help a bit with that,' he said.

'What happened at the storage unit?' said DS Stanford.

'Well, I checked box 623 and it was empty.'

'Why did you parade in so triumphantly then?' said DC Murphy.

'I'm getting to it!' said DC North. 'You've broken my flow now. Anyway. The box was empty, but when I spoke to the receptionist, he said there had been frequent visitors to the box over the past month or so, but in short bursts, usually over a period of a few days each time.'

'Definitely sounds like a drop site of some sort then,' said DCI Melrose. 'How did they access the box though? Wouldn't they have needed a key?'

‘Nope. It has keypad access. All they’d need is a code,’ said DC North. ‘There’s more as well. You know when I spoke to them before and they told me that the contract for the box had been taken out in Max Roberts’ name?’

‘Let me guess – it wasn’t Max Roberts,’ said DC Murphy.

‘What? How did you know that?’

‘Autopsy results,’ said DC Murphy. ‘He had rheumatoid arthritis. There’s no way he could fire a gun, let alone push Professor Hail over the balcony, which also casts doubt on his involvement in the rest of this. We’re now working on the theory that he was a scapegoat or had a partner.’

DC North dropped his backpack down on the floor.

‘Well, that stole my thunder a bit,’ he said.

‘But why risk being caught by putting the stolen items on a public auction site?’ said DS Stanford.

‘Well, if the partner or the real person behind all this thought we were getting close, then pinning the evidence to Max is a good way to get us off the trail,’ said DCI Melrose.

‘Hang on a minute, DC North. If you know it wasn’t Max Roberts who opened the account does that mean you know who did?’ said DS Stanford.

‘Yes and no.’

‘What does that mean?’ said DS Stanford.

‘Yes, I know who rented the storage box, but no, I don’t know who it was.’

‘OK, can we skip the cryptic clues?’ said DCI Melrose. ‘What exactly are you trying to say?’

‘The account was taken out in Max Roberts’ name, but it wasn’t actually opened by him.’

‘Yes, that much is clear. Who was it opened by

then?' said DS Stanford.

'It was opened by his wife.'

'But Max wasn't married,' said DC Murphy.

'Exactly!' said DC North.

'Any CCTV of her signing up?' said DS Stanford.

'Yes, but you only ever see her from behind and she's wearing a hat that covers her entire head. Here, I grabbed a photo of her handing back the signed contract.'

DCI Melrose looked over to DS Stanford and raised her eyebrows.

'I know who our killer is.'

29

'DCI Melrose here. Everyone in position? Over.'

'DS Stanford here. Inside loading bay. Over.'

'Sergeant Brooks here. Armed response team leader. We are in position. Over.'

'DC North here. Outside loading bay. Over.'

'DC Murphy here. Covering main entrance to museum. Over.'

'OK, everyone, hold your positions and wait on my command. We need to make sure they unload the items first. DCI Melrose, over.'

A lorry began reversing towards the loading bay. When it had pulled to a stop, two men climbed down from the cab and walked to the rear of the truck.

'Hey? Is anyone there?' said the driver.

'Yes, Frank, I'm here,' said Georgie, emerging from between a stack of crates.

'Everyone gone?' said Frank.

'Yes, the museum is locked up for the night. Only Jeremy, the security guard, is onsite, but he won't bother us here, don't worry.'

'It sounds as though the couriers are involved in this as well. Hold positions a bit longer. DCI Melrose, over.'

'Large shipment you've got here,' said Frank. 'Must be a big exhibition this time.'

Georgie laughed.

'Yeah, the biggest one yet, I reckon.'

'You not worried about the heat from the dead Professor?'

'Didn't you hear? I've taken care of all that, Frank. We've got an open channel here now. Come on, let's get it all unloaded. I don't want to spend my whole evening here.'

Frank lowered the tailgate until it rested upon the concrete surface of the loading bay and with the help of his companion, they began to unload the truck, pallet by pallet.

Suddenly, DC North lost his footing and his leg slipped down the damp mound of grass he had been standing on, knocking a discarded beer bottle over.

'What the fuck was that?' said Frank, dropping the handle of the pallet trolley.

'Came from over there,' said Georgie. 'You got a torch?'

Frank shuffled back along the side of the truck and opened the cab door, grabbing a light from underneath the seat, before returning to the loading bay.

'Here.'

Georgie took the torch and began to shine it towards the group of bins that DC North had taken refuge behind. The young detective constable was frozen to the spot, his heart thumping in his chest. In the darkness, he saw something scurry from beneath him and run across in front of the lorry. Georgie tracked the creature with the beam of light.

'It's just a rat, Frank, jeez. Let's stop wasting time.'

'OK team. Move in on the count of three. One. Two. Three. Go, go, go.'

'Police! Stay where you are and put your hands

behind your heads!'

Before Georgie and the couriers could move, they had been blocked from all directions. DS Stanford, DC North and DC Murphy stepped forward and placed the suspects in handcuffs.

'What the hell is going on?' said Georgie.

'Well, why don't we take a look?' said DCI Melrose, walking across to one of the crates.

She placed her hand inside and pulled out an ornamental wooden box.

'Careful with that, don't you know how old that is?' said Georgie. 'You can't just pick these items up; they have to be handled by experts.'

'I'm sure they do,' said DCI Melrose.

The detective began tapping the box methodically, until she heard a hollow sound. She prised away a small panel, revealing several passports hidden inside.

'What the hell are they doing in there?' said Georgie. 'I don't know anything about those.'

'Me neither,' said Frank. 'Look, we just pick up the items and deliver them. We're just the couriers, we're not mixed up in any of this.'

'You were never in a relationship with Professor Hail, that was a lie. You weren't breaking up in the café. He was telling you that he was going to expose you, wasn't he?' said DCI Melrose, standing face to face with Georgie.

There was silence.

'He'd found out you were using the museum transport for smuggling. He even ordered a fake passport and birth certificate as evidence and that's the first time you realised he was on to you. And that's when you knew that he'd have to die to protect your secret. But first, you needed to set something else in motion. An insurance policy. You befriended

Max at work, preying on his loneliness. And when he confided in you about his financial worries, you pounced and began to orchestrate the burglaries. You used them as a smokescreen for murder, knowing that eventually, the evidence would point to Max.'

Georgie stared straight ahead, avoiding any eye contact with DCI Melrose. The detective moved in even closer.

'I'm guessing he called you after we released him on bail. Looking for a friend. Probably scared as hell. Never done anything wrong in his life before. Instead of helping him, you broke into my house and planted his badge, assaulting me in the process. Then, you lured Max to his allotment and murdered him in cold blood. All because of your greed.'

Georgie remained quiet.

'I bet he didn't tell you about the arthritis, did he?'

Georgie twitched slightly.

'That's right. He had arthritis. And that's going to prove he couldn't have fired the gun that killed him. Nor could he have pushed Professor Hail over the balcony. That was all you. You've got a heart of stone, you utter bitch.'

DCI Melrose took a few steps back.

'Read them their rights and place them under arrest. Then get them the hell out of my sight.'

30

DCI Melrose, DS Stanford and DC Murphy sat on a bench along the promenade, watching DC North attempting to cross the main road whilst cradling several bundles of paper bags and cans of fizzy drinks in his arms.

'Do you think we should help him?' said DC Murphy.

'He's fine,' said DCI Melrose, raising a smile.

'Being a detective is all about multitasking,' laughed DS Stanford.

The sound of a horn from a passing car rang out as it sped by the detective constable, who eventually found a big enough gap to run across to where the rest of his team were sat, barely hiding their amusement.

'Thanks for the help!' said DC North.

'You seemed to have it under control,' said DS Stanford.

'Hmm. It wasn't even my idea to get fish and chips,' said DC North. 'I wanted pizza. They're easier to carry as well, I reckon.'

'This is DCI Melrose's first successful case in her new home by the sea,' said DC Murphy. 'And nothing embodies the seaside experience more than a bag of proper, locally sourced fish and chips.'

'Claire, we're off duty now, call me Kate. Joseph, Jack, that goes for you too. No titles out of the workplace, please.'

The team smiled in acknowledgement, as Joseph began to hand out the food and drink.

'I just wanted to say thank you for welcoming me,' said Kate, opening her drink and holding up the can. 'It's always a bit scary moving somewhere new, but you've helped me feel at home. Well done and thank you for all your hard work on this case and here's to solving many more.'

'Hear, hear!' said Jack, as the group tapped their cans together.

'Be careful of the seagulls,' said Claire. 'They've got a bit of a reputation here for pinching food.'

'They won't get any of mine,' said Joseph. 'I'm starving!'

'What would you normally do after solving a case in London?' said Jack.

'A lot of paperwork,' laughed Kate.

'Did you not have any post-case rituals then?' said Jack.

'Well, there was a pub we would usually go to, tucked away down one of those smelly side alleys. There would never be any seats left though, so we'd usually end up congregating outside. They did the most amazing pie and mash. Not the easiest thing to eat whilst you're standing up with a bottle of beer clamped between your knees.'

'Perhaps we should make fish and chips our post-case ritual,' said Claire.

'Or pizza,' said Joseph.

'How about we just all agree to come and sit on this bench?' said Jack. 'After every case, we all gather here and just talk.'

'I'd like that very much,' smiled Kate.

'And if there happens to be pizza, then so be it,'

said Joseph.

'Oh, shush!' said Claire, throwing one of her chips in his direction.

'Great! You've done it now!' said Joseph, watching as a seagull swooped in and grabbed the piece of food from the ground.

Jack stood up and stamped his feet a few times, which was enough to usher the seagulls back onto the railings on the opposite side of the promenade.

'What are you all doing with your days off tomorrow?' said Kate. 'Any nice plans?'

'Seeing my boyfriend,' said Claire. 'He's going to teach me how to paddleboard.'

'Good weather for it tomorrow,' said Joseph. 'The sea is going to be calm, according to reports. I'm going to be visiting my parents. They live about 30 miles along the coast.'

'Getting your washing done again?' joked Jack.

'You take your dirty clothes back home to have them washed?' said Kate.

'Well, my washing machine doesn't work,' said Joseph, defensively.

'That broke a year ago!' said Claire. 'You still haven't got that fixed?'

'Look, I'm really doing it for my mum, OK? She misses having me around, so me taking my washing back every now and then, well, it's so she doesn't feel like I've completely flown the nest.'

'That's the most ridiculous thing I've ever heard,' said Claire, pretending to throw another chip.

'What about you, Jack? Any plans?' said Kate.

'Taking Bailey down to the local park to kick a ball around. I reckon he'll be playing for England one day.'

'He's good, is he?' said Claire.

'Well, you know sometimes in games you might hold back a bit, because you're a full-grown adult and they're just a kid? Yeah, the difference is I'm not holding back when I'm playing against Bailey. I'm trying to win, but he's so good that I lose all the time.'

'There, there, granddad,' joked Joseph. 'How about you, Kate? Your first official day off in our lovely town. Assuming there isn't another murder!'

'I still haven't unpacked, so I want to get everything sorted at the house. And I should spend some time with Chester. I've barely seen him since we moved here. I'm worried he'll start scratching all the furniture and playing up if he thinks I've abandoned him.'

'Chester's a cat, right?' said Joseph, laughing.

'Yes, sorry, he's my cat. Here's a picture of him.'

'Aww, he's adorable,' said Claire. 'I've always wanted a cat, but they don't allow them in the place I'm renting at the moment.'

'That's such a shame. Chester is a very good companion. I picked him up as a kitten from a rescue centre about 5 years ago now. I think he'll enjoy living here in a house with a garden more than our old flat in London.'

'How did he get in and out of the flat?' said Jack.

'He was a bit of a celebrity,' joked Kate. 'Everyone in our block knew him and probably fed him as well. I would let him out when I was leaving for work and then when he wanted to get back in, he'd sit at the main door until one of the other residents let him in. I'd put a little cat flap in my front door and he had a sensor attached to his collar that opened it.'

'Sounds like a character,' smiled Claire.

‘He is. Loyal too. He’s always ready with a cuddle when I’ve had a bad day at work, or just been discharged from hospital.’

Kate realised what she had said and stopped talking.

‘Hospital?’ said Joseph.

‘Have you been in hospital quite a bit then?’ said Claire.

‘No, no, I mean, you know, the odd time I’ve had to go into hospital. You know, a procedure here and there.’

‘I don’t think it’s our place to pry,’ said Jack, noticing Kate’s discomfort at the direction the conversation had taken. ‘I would’ve helped you with all the boxes if I hadn’t promised Bailey a game.’

‘That’s kind of you, thank you. I’m sure I’ll manage fine. Plus, I reckon my neighbour, Rachel, wouldn’t mind stepping in if I need any assistance. She’s been so lovely to me.’

‘She’s one of the receptionist’s friends, isn’t she?’ said Joseph.

‘Yes, that’s right.’

‘Such a shame about her son,’ said Claire.

‘I remember working that case,’ said Jack. ‘Alex his name was. Poor little guy. Terrible thing to happen to anyone.’

‘I clumsily dropped his picture when I was in her house,’ said Kate. ‘Even worse than that, I stupidly asked what happened to him.’

‘Did she tell you?’ said Jack.

‘No. I felt terrible, so I started talking about something else. What did happen to Alex?’

‘He drowned,’ said Jack. ‘Two years ago.’

‘Well, I feel even more terrible about breaking the picture now.’

‘He went out sailing one day with her ex-husband, Tim,’ said Jack. ‘They were about a mile from shore when the sky turned. Within minutes, a storm had rolled in across the bay.’

‘They turned the boat around and began to head back to the harbour,’ said Claire. ‘Suddenly, the boat capsized and they were thrown into the sea. Tim was able to fire a distress flare and the lookout at the lifeboat station spotted it.’

‘By the time they reached them, they could only see Tim, struggling to keep his head above water,’ said Jack. ‘They did a search, but the waves were so violent they had to head back in. They sent a helicopter out later in the afternoon when everything had calmed down, but they never found Alex’s body.’

‘That’s awful,’ said Kate. ‘Is that why they divorced?’

‘Their marriage couldn’t survive that,’ said Jack. ‘I don’t think Rachel will ever forgive him.’

‘Thank you for telling me,’ said Kate. ‘I can only imagine how difficult the last two years have been for Rachel. And that can’t have been easy for you, working the case. After time, you find yourself woven more and more into the fabric of a place, don’t you? Thread by thread. With every investigation you take on.’

‘I can remember my first murder case,’ said Claire. ‘I can remember it as if it had happened yesterday.’

‘I don’t think you ever forget them,’ said Kate.

‘I couldn’t go in to begin with, when I arrived at my first crime scene,’ said Joseph. ‘Must’ve been stood outside for a good 5 minutes.’

‘It affects everyone differently,’ said Jack. ‘Doesn’t mean you’re weak. Just human.’

‘What?’ said Joseph. ‘Oh, no, I don’t mean like

that. I meant because I couldn't get those stupid gloves on. I was blowing in them and everything.'

The group descended into laughter. It was the break in the conversation that they all needed. A chance, amongst all the gloom, to embrace the lighter side.

Kate sat back, the smile still resting upon her face. Although she felt more tired than she'd ever felt before, in that moment she was also content.

A new job. A new town. A new start.

Printed in Great Britain
by Amazon

79958673R00140